WATCH THIS SPACE

Out to Launch

Sch $14.00

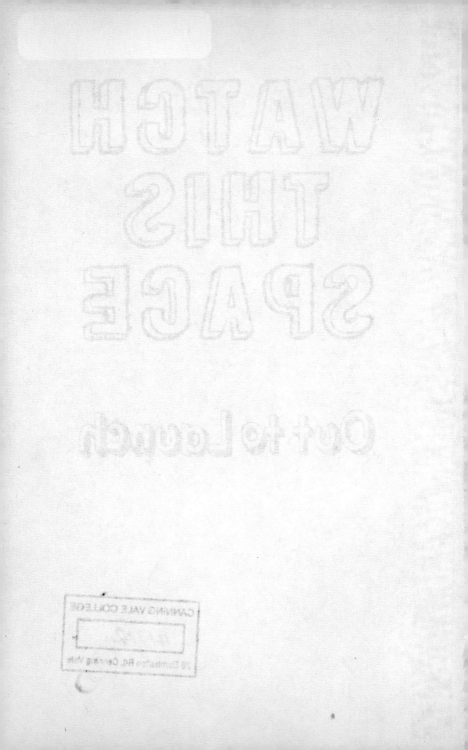

WATCH THIS SPACE

Out to Launch

Colin Thompson

illustrations by the author

RANDOM HOUSE AUSTRALIA

This work is fictitious. Any resemblance to anyone living or dead is an amazing coincidence and if you do actually recognise yourself then you are probably living on the Planet Janet and are advised to keep it to yourself.

A Random House book
Published by Random House Australia Pty Ltd
Level 3, 100 Pacific Highway, North Sydney NSW 2060
www.randomhouse.com.au

Penguin
Random House
RANDOM HOUSE BOOKS

First published by Random House Australia in 2015

Random House Books is part of the Penguin Random House group of companies whose addresses can be found at global.penguinrandomhouse.com.

National Library of Australia
Cataloguing-in-Publication Entry

Creator: Thompson, Colin (Colin Edward), author
Title: Watch this space / Colin Thompson
ISBN: 9781742756202 (pbk)
Target Audience: For primary school age
Subjects: Space colonies – Juvenile fiction
          Interplanetary voyages – Juvenile fiction
Dewey Number: A823.3

Design, illustrations, typesetting by Colin Thompson
Additional typesetting by Midland Typesetters, Australia
Printed in Australia by Griffin Press, an accredited ISO AS/NZS 14001:2004
Environmental Management System printer

Random House Australia uses papers that are natural, renewable and recyclable products and made from wood grown in sustainable forests. The logging and manufacturing processes are expected to conform to the environmental regulations of the country of origin.

10 9 8 7 6

If you have ever gone outside on a moonlit night, laid down on the grass[1] and looked up at the stars and thought, 'Um, er, I wonder if there's life out there with like, er, tiny bodies and huge eyes and, like, massive brains and superpowers or whatever,' or something equally deep and meaningless, then this book is for you.

If you haven't ever done that, then it's about time you did.

---

[1] *It has to be grass. Concrete is too hard and you won't be able to concentrate on the sky. Earth is too wet and will make you want to go to the toilet.*

PROLOGUE

On Monday morning a notice appeared in every newspaper, on every TV, in everyone's inbox and, just to make sure no-one missed out, billions of pieces of paper floated down from the sky in every country of the world.[2]

The announcement said:

---

[2] *Not even anyone as far away as Tristan da Cunha and that little outside toilet halfway up Mount Everest would have missed it, unless the little outside toilet had run out of paper and someone had used the notice as a substitute without reading it first.*

WOULD YOU LIKE TO BE THE MOST FAMOUS FAMILY EVER?

And we mean EVER!!

FORGET ABOUT GOING ON TV AND PRETENDING YOU'VE GOT TALENT. WE ALL KNOW YOU HAVEN'T.

FORGET ABOUT 'DANCING WITH THE NOBODIES'. WE ALL KNOW YOU'VE GOT LESS RHYTHM THAN A POTATO.

FORGET ABOUT 'AT HOME WITH THE DESPERATE LOSERS OF HAPPY VALLEY', WHICH YOU ONLY WATCH BECAUSE IT MAKES YOU FEEL LESS OF A LOSER YOURSELF.

THIS IS THE BIG ONE!!
BIGGER THAN BIG!!
BIGGER THAN YOUR SAD LITTLE IMAGINATION!!

NO-ONE WILL EVER BE MORE FAMOUS!!

ABSOLUTELY NO TALENT REQUIRED!!

On the back of the paper there was a whole lot of boring stuff, terms and conditions about how you had to be a family consisting of one mum, one dad, one or more boys and one or more girls and maybe a really old granny and possibly a pet of some sort, as long as it wasn't as big as a pony. Hundreds of losers complained that it discriminated against them because they didn't have a partner or children and/or a dog or a cat. Those people all got an email that read:

The reason you haven't got a partner is because you are a pathetic whingeing loser. So let us all give thanks that you haven't got a partner who you might well bore to death.

This message, of course, caused an even bigger uproar, but because there were only a few hundred complainers, no-one had any sympathy for them and locked as many of them as they could in small dark cupboards with all the alternative organic vegetarians, who were also forbidden to apply.

The flyer also explained that the winning family would be shown LIVE on television EVERY WEEKEND and the WHOLE WORLD would watch them being the MOST FAMOUS people ever. It didn't actually tell the winning family where they would be or what they'd be doing, but hey, FAMOUS, FAMOUS, FAMOUS.

They got one hundred and fifteen million applications, which was one hundred and fourteen million more than their wildest dreams told them they might possibly get.

So the next message said:

There will be a short delay.

When it gradually sank in just how many people one hundred and fifteen million was, the TV company sent a follow-up email with the exact same message but missing the word 'short'.

When they realised that each of the one hundred and fifteen million application forms

covered a family of at least four people, they sent a third message.

Due to the wonderful enthusiasm such huge numbers of you have shown, we are currently unable to tell you when the finalists will be announced.

The message went on to explain that a lot more people had applied than had been anticipated so could everyone please be patient until they heard further. The message ended with the inspired sentence that went on to become the most famous sentence in the whole of television history and the title of the show itself:

WATCH THIS SPACE

It had all started about three years earlier, with the most fantastic idea ever for a reality TV show. They would put an ordinary family on the moon – not scientists or astronauts, but a nice family like what you and I have, who everyone could identify with, so the whole world would feel like they were part of it all.

Watch This Space would be the ultimate reality TV show, guaranteed to break records, with ratings that would leave the producers of all other shows weeping in the dust. Each week everyone would tune in to see the lunar pioneers living their incredible, groundbreaking, exciting lives. Nothing anyone would come up with in the future would ever be able to top it.

The show was the brainchild of Radius Limpfast, a superstar producer in the world of reality television and the owner of the global entertainment corporation LIMP-TV. It was Radius who had invented two of the decade's biggest shows, *Hey, Hey, Fatty Bum Bum*[3] and *The Slax Factor*,[4] which had made him a billionaire several times over and chairman of the world's most powerful television station, which, of course, was nearly all owned by Radius Limpfast too.

---

[3] *Where eight normal-sized contestants were fed a super-diet of high-fat meat pies and deep-fried banana thickshakes over a period of twelve weeks. The contestant who had grown the fattest bottom in that time got a brand-new house with extra-wide doors and a lifetime supply of Lardo's Finest Pies.* Hey, Hey, Fatty Bum Bum *had been a phenomenal success and when one of the contestants had actually exploded live on TV, the ratings had gone through the roof.*

[4] *This show had been aimed at the more discerning viewer, and featured a very glamorous but serious (she wore glasses) reporter who travelled the world taking the mickey out of people's terrible trousers. This, of course, resulted in huge sales of really dreadful nylon tracksuits to people who wanted to be on TV.*

To everyone who worked for him, from his top producers to the trainee toilet-seat polisher, Radius Limpfast was known as 'RR', which he used because it also stood for Rolls-Royce, the greatest and poshest car to exist. When it was pointed out to him that his initials were actually 'RL', not 'RR', he changed his name to Radius Radius Limpfast.

'No-one will ever top this show,' Radius told his board members. 'Not in a million years.'

'But how much is it going to cost?' the accountants asked.

'Billions,' said Radius Limpfast. 'Lots of billions. But it will be peanuts compared to how much it will make. And,' he added, 'by my calculations, we will make all our money back before our winning family even leaves Earth.'

Everyone who worked at LIMP-TV agreed with everything Radius Limpfast said, even when they didn't. Radius Limpfast was that sort of person – which didn't so much mean that his staff adored him and thought he could do no wrong as it meant that anyone who disagreed with him,

even over something as small as how many lumps of sugar made the best-tasting coffee, usually found themselves either being suddenly out of work or being a contestant in the grossest reality shows, the latest one being number two in the ratings, which was very apt as it was called *Number Twos* and involved two teams, two rows of very dirty lavatories and two very small toothbrushes.

So no-one asked the obvious question: 'Won't it get boring watching these people stuck in a glass dome, week after week, on a dead rock with no life or plants or anything?'

Of course, if they'd said that, Radius would have replied: 'I've got a few little things that will liven it up.'

So everyone had agreed that *Watch This Space* was a totally brilliant idea and that there was no way anything could go wrong.

'Unless we want it to,' said Radius, with a knowing smile.

Radius Limpfast did a lot of knowing smiles. It reassured people that he was on top of things and had

planned for every eventuality. What it actually meant was that he was a very, very clever conman, who so far had managed to stay one step ahead of disaster, mostly because lots of the disasters had been his own inventions created to make his shows more popular.

'While the engineers are building the spaceship to get our family to the moon, we will hold worldwide auditions to find the right family,' he said.

'And,' he added, 'a crack team of Patagonian engineers are building the ultimate robot to go along with our family and to maintain the spaceship. After all, we don't want our family running out of food or oxygen and dying horribly, do we?'

Which meant, 'We don't want them running out of food or oxygen and dying horribly as long as the show is top of the ratings.' And as Radius Limpfast's life was governed by the cash register, he had already worked out the cost difference between bringing them all safely back to Earth and letting them die horribly on the moon.

The TV station was overwhelmed. People didn't just write, ring and email to apply, but they actually

turned up at the TV studios, tens of thousands of them, some having travelled across continents to get there.

It was chaos. The people who worked there couldn't get into the station, even with hundreds of police and security guards clearing the roads for miles around. The only way they could keep the station running was to bring staff in by helicopter and, once they were in, they had to stay there.

'Brilliant!' said Radius Limpfast as he stood in his penthouse office, looking down at the crowds that stretched as far as the eye could see. 'I told you we'd make a profit before we even launched.'

'Fantastic,' said his right-hand man, who was actually a right-hand woman called Fiona Hardly, who was, in fact, left-handed. 'How? Advertising?'

'Nope,' said Radius. 'Every single applicant is paying for an official application form and, by the way things are looking, the five million forms we printed aren't going to be nearly enough.'

'OMG, RR, you are a genius.'

A rumour started that there were not enough

application forms for everyone and eBay was brought to a halt with people selling application forms, most of which were fake. The world went *Watch This Space* crazy, and it felt as if the whole thing had taken on a life of its own, which was exactly what Radius Limpfast wanted. By the end of the second week, Radius Limpfast was the richest, the second-richest and the third-richest person in the world.

Sorting that many forms would have taken years, so over ninety per cent of them were secretly converted into a very big bonfire in a very remote valley in Patagonia. The TV station's Top Cleverest Science/Maths Person, Professor Smallparts,[5] calculated that by the time they'd manage to interview one hundred and fifteen million applicants and their families, quite a lot of them would probably have died of old age.

---

[5] *To save time with university and studying, Professor Smallparts had changed his first name from 'Terry' to 'Professor' by deed poll. Radius Limpfast knew this, but that was just the sort of devious cunning he admired in his employees, especially when he could pay them a lot less because they weren't properly qualified.*

'We need a shortcut,' said Radius Limpfast. 'We've got masses of technology. Surely you can come up with something to eliminate the millions of families we all know would be totally useless?'

Professor Smallparts thought about it. Being a scientist as well as being a TV executive meant he'd soon come up with a great list of ideas. The trouble was, the very qualities that had got him the job at LIMP-TV – a very sharp mind and no moral scruples – meant that most of his ideas were terminally dangerous and illegal.

'Oh well,' said Professor Smallparts, feeding pages and pages of brilliant, original and creative dead-making ideas into the paper shredder. 'Back to the chopping block. Oops, sorry, back to the drawing board.'

It took a while, but eventually Professor Smallparts came up with a solution. It involved a camera and some clever software, which was referred to by Radius's office as the Moron Machine or, to be precise, the Moron Machines, as they'd built a lot of them. The machines were taken to all the major

cities around the world, and fresh messages were sent out telling applicants where to go and when.

'Basically, in the blink of an eye, the computer will filter out all the unsuitable people,' said Professor Smallparts.

'By "unsuitable",' said Radius, 'I assume you mean anyone who is too ugly, too nerdy, too fat, too scary...'

It took over an hour for Radius to get through his 'unsuitable' list, which he'd written down when he had first dreamt up this reality show.

'And there are other people who you might think would be just what we want, but are actually unsuitable too,' he added. 'For example, if the father is too ugly it's obvious we won't want him, but if he's too handsome we won't want him either.'

'Why not?' said Fiona.

'Well, the women would adore him, so the men would be jealous and hate him,' Radius explained. 'Same if he's too clever. Let's be honest, most of our viewers are thick. Sorry, I meant to say ALL our viewers are thick. If they weren't, they

wouldn't be watching the wonderful garbage that is making us rich. Their stupidity is the reason they love all our shows. It makes them feel intelligent because they are more intelligent than the idiots we put on their screens.'

'But that means we've got to choose a total brain-dead zombie,' said Fiona.

'Mmm, that won't work either. He could end up killing them all, which would make for brilliant TV, but probably a very short series – though of course we could then have a spin-off series with the police going to the moon,' said Radius. 'No, we need our man to be ordinary, pleasant-looking with just a touch of loser, who makes silly mistakes in the sort of way that will endear him to everyone.'

'But you can't put a bunch of idiots on the moon,' said Professor. 'Even if the entire space station is totally automated, it will need at least one person with a bit of intelligence to keep an eye on it all, otherwise the entire family could be dead within a week.'

'That's why we're going to send a super-clever robot with them,' said Radius.

In the end, it was agreed that the wife could be a lot more intelligent than the husband (while not making him feel stupid) as long as it was in an endearing way, too.

'Because women viewers won't be jealous of her,' said Radius. 'They will identify with her.'

So Professor Smallparts worked on his computer to tweak the software to pick out exactly the right male and female candidates.

'And the children,' said Radius. 'Ideally, the boy should be the younger of the two, a sort of clone of his dad, say about ten years old, and the daughter, say about fourteen, should be like her mum – and it would be great if she could be the cleverest one in the family. Nice bit of potential infighting there – daughter rebelling against mum, brother resenting clever sister, dad taking daughter's side – oh yes, I can see it all.'

Fiona wrote down all of Radius's instructions.

'So, Professor, can you get your Moron Machines to pick a family with all those qualities?' Radius asked.

'Absolutely,' Professor lied. 'Probably take a week or so, though.'

Of course there was one potential problem that no-one dared talk about. Suppose they found the perfect man, but his wife was awful? Or the wife was exactly what they were looking for, but the husband was useless? Radius Limpfast had thought of this, but before he considered making any plans that might involve using a husband and wife who had never actually met each other before and maybe having to sort of kill off their partners,[6] he reckoned that with so many applicants there was a good chance they would find a suitable husband and wife who were already married to each other.

So that solves that, he thought.

In the end, though, the family were chosen almost by chance. In the boardroom there was a wall of large TV monitors, tuned in to all the different LIMP-TV stations round the world. There was also

---

[6] *He did actually have a well-organised plan that could do this. It was filed away in his very, extremely top-secret Safe of Last Resorts.*

a row of screens relaying live pictures of the crowds queueing up around the TV studios.

Radius idly scanned the boring lines of hopefuls.

'We need a shortcut,' he said, half-watching the screen. 'We all know that there are probably tens of thousands of families out there who'd be all right and I know the Moron Machines are doing a brilliant job, but we haven't got time to go through every single one of them.'

On the other hand, he said to himself, *we want every single one of them to think that they've been considered, otherwise we could have the biggest riot in history on our hands.*

'Yes, RR,' said Fiona Hardly, 'but we don't want anyone to think they haven't been considered, otherwise we could have the biggest riot in history on our hands.'

I should marry this woman, Radius Limpfast thought.

He had always avoided getting married in case it all went wrong and he had to give some of his money away, but in Fiona Hardly he saw someone

19

who had so much in common with him – they were like reflections of each other and your reflection is something you spend your whole life with and with which you are usually deeply in love.[7]

He also thought, *Mega-riots – I wonder if there's a series in that?*

'Especially those disgusting dags out there with their tracksuits and bags of chips,' Fiona added. 'We don't want crowds of them rioting everywhere.'

Radius nodded. Those disgusting dags were his most loyal viewers and he was making yet another fortune from his fleet of fast-food vans moving through the crowds selling them the chips.

'Might make a good reality series, though,' Fiona said. 'And,' she added, as she knew on which side her bread was buttered, '*Watch This Space* has to be the most brilliant name for a series ever.'

---

[7] *Unless your reflection is hideous and gross, but then those people usually avoid mirrors or live under rocks, only coming out after dark to go shopping in those creepy weird supermarkets that stay open all night. I know about this because I've seen them.*

Radius Limpfast wanted to throw his arms round Fiona and tell her she was a genius and that he was head over heels in love with her and wanted to spend the rest of his life with her for a very long time or even longer and would she marry him tomorrow – well, not so much tomorrow, but as soon as they had a prenuptial agreement agreed upon and signed.[8] But he didn't. It wasn't that Radius didn't want to act anything less than super-cool in front of the other board members because it might slightly undermine his authority, which was true, but the real reason was that deep down inside he was shy and his feelings were confusing him. He hardly knew that the word 'shy' even existed, never mind ever having felt that way before. So he just acted like Mr Cool.

'Interesting,' Radius said. 'It was, of course, on top of my list of titles and hearing someone else say it just confirms it.'

---

[8] *A prenuptial agreement is a contract a couple sign before they get married. It means that if the couple end up getting divorced, the richer one of the two gets to keep it all for themselves.*

Suddenly Radius spotted the perfect face in the crowd below.

'Camera six,' he called into a microphone, 'quick, pan right and follow the guy in the green jacket.'

'Look at him,' he said to Fiona and the other board members. 'He looks perfect and so do his wife and two kids. Can't see a granny, but we'll worry about that later. Go down and get them.'

Apart from the green jacket, which was more of a sort of grey colour, the guy did look perfect – not too self-confident, not too good-looking, nice, clean and tidy – and although years of reality TV had given Radius a keen eye for people, experience also told him that someone who looked perfect could sometimes be the worst choice ever.

Still, we have to start somewhere, Radius said to himself. *There's no way we've got time to audition every applicant. And his wife looks good too.*

So it was that Stark Contrast, his wife, Laura, and their two children were pulled out of the obscurity of the crowd and brought into the world of legends and fame.

As Stark himself said later in one of his rare jokes, 'It was one small step for the Contrasts and one giant step for um, er, us' – which, as jokes went, was rubbish.

Introducing RADIUS LIMPFAST

Radius Limpfast has been creating his life story ever since he was five years old, when he discovered that a bit of creative lying could make life much, much better in so many different ways.

Such a discovery means that he has never let things like the truth or the facts get in the way of a life that millions envy and admire. Reality has been mangled up and buried so deeply that people can't even agree how tall Radius actually is. If anyone asks the question, 'What is Radius like? – meaning, 'How tall is he?' or 'Is he good-looking?' or 'How old is he?' – the answer is usually, 'Well, you know, sort of, er, you know.'

Because Radius is famous, there are a lot of photos of him – except they aren't actually of him because he employs several doubles who look nothing like him. Radius is a confused mixture of someone who loves being rich and famous and someone who wants to be anonymous, which, of course, is almost impossible.

His parents have been many, many people, from mysterious European royals to gypsies, circus

performers, famous politicians, actors, inventors and dark mysterious beings who could even have come from a galaxy far, far away. So varied and so convincing are his stories that there are times when even his own mother has wondered if she is actually related to him.

All evidence – including the actual body – of his father was lost in a Very Suspicious Fire, which started in Radius's own nursery when he was seven, spread rapidly to all the family photo albums, passports and birth certificates, but magically avoided destroying any of the money and cheques that were stored in the very same safe.

The family retainer was accused of arson, but nothing was proved. And no-one suspected the angelic little seven-year-old when boxes of matches and lighter fuel were found buried under his toy soldiers, together with a copy of *The Boys' Book of Arson*.

iona and three security guards went down to the street to fetch the Contrasts. Radius told them to make it look like the family were in some sort of trouble so as not to make the crowds suspicious.

'Excuse me,' Fiona said, 'could you come with me, please? There seems to be a problem with your application forms.'

'What?' said the man as he and his wife, son and daughter followed Fiona through a small, inconspicuous door in the side of the building.

No-one else in the queue suspected anything was happening. The people behind the Contrasts were delighted because they'd moved up one space in the queue, and the people in front of the Contrasts

didn't care because they were already in front of them.

'Sorry about that,' said Fiona, once the Contrasts were safely inside the elevator. 'We didn't want to upset the crowd by letting them think you'd been chosen.'

'But we haven't,' said Laura Contrast, the mother.

'Well, I think you probably have,' said Fiona.

'That's ridiculous,' said the daughter, Primrose Contrast. 'We've haven't done anything, like an audition or stuff.'

'Plenty of time for all that,' said Radius as the family walked into the boardroom.

He explained that the response to the invitation had been so massively overwhelming that if they went through all the procedures they'd planned for every applicant, by the time they'd finish, Radius himself would be over ninety-nine years old, instead of the thirty-seven he was now.

'So we had to slim down the selection procedure,' he said.

'What, you mean, by picking us out of the crowd at random?' said Primrose, who was obviously the sharpest one in the family.

'Yes, but why us?' said Stark Contrast, who was obviously the unsharpest one in the family.

'Yeah, wow,' said Jack Contrast, who was a bit sharper than his father, but a lot duller than his sister.

Laura Contrast said nothing, nor did the expression on her face give anything away that told Radius and Fiona exactly where she fitted into the family sharpness-wise.

Both Radius Limpfast and Fiona Hardly made mental notes and came to similar conclusions. The daughter would be the only one who might be a problem, but then problems always make reality TV shows more interesting. And a few extra problems could easily be created.

'Yeah, right,' said Primrose.

'It's true,' said Radius, 'except the selection process wasn't exactly random.'

'Mmm, thought so,' said Primrose.

'You, dear people,' Radius said, 'were chosen

because you stood out from the crowd like stars. And stars are what you are going to be – superstars, even.'

Stark and Jack were gobsmacked, over the moon, excited and speechless, apart from a few wows and yeahs. Laura was pretty excited too, but said nothing.

But Primrose was suspicious. A voice inside her head kept telling her that it would all end in tears, but another voice said, *Oh, what the hell, it sure beats school*.

'OK,' said Radius, 'let's get out of here.'

'What?' said Stark. 'We're leaving already?'

'Well, no,' Fiona explained, 'not for the moon. They haven't finished building the ship yet. No, we're going to the country so we can get to know you better and organise all the training and that sort of stuff.'

'Moon?' said Primrose. 'What do you mean – moon?'

'Oh, didn't we tell you?' said Radius. 'You're going to live on the moon.'

'Don't be ridiculous,' said Primrose. 'You can't live on the moon.'

'We're building a luxury home up there,' Fiona said. 'It'll be amazing.'

'Yeah,' Radius continued, 'and we're building a state-of-the-art spaceship to take you there.'

'No way,' said Primrose.

'No way,' said Jack and his dad.

'Um,' Laura said because she was so overwhelmed she couldn't think of anything else.

'Wow!' said Jack and his dad. 'Wow.'

'Exactly,' said Radius. 'So now we're going to whisk you away to a luxury secret location and get you ready to meet the world's press.'

'What about Crumley?' said Jack.

'Crumbly?' said Fiona. 'What on Earth is crumbly?'

'Our dog,' Primrose said. 'And he's called *Crumley*, not crumbly. We can't just go off and leave with no-one to look after him. Not that I'm going anyway.'

'I think you'll find you are,' said Radius.

'I think you'll find I'm not,' Primrose snapped back.

'You signed the application form, didn't you?' said Fiona.

'No, my parents did,' said Primrose. 'I wouldn't sign it.'

'Irrelevant,' Radius said and smiled. 'At your age, your parents decide what you're going to do, not you. So we'll send someone to get your dog.'

Before Primrose could protest, Fiona made a phone call, took the Contrasts' house keys and someone went off to collect Crumley.

'Can he come with us?' said Jack.

'Absolutely,' said Radius. 'We're going to my house in the country. He'll love it there. There's woods and fields and rabbits, loads of them. He'll have a brilliant time.'

'I meant to the moon,' said Jack.

Big lights flashed inside Radius Limpfast's head. *A perfect-looking family AND a dog – brilliant*, he thought.

Fiona made a note to organise a dog spacesuit. *There's a documentary in that*, she thought.

Radius Limpfast was right. *Watch This Space*

was going to be the greatest TV series in history for years and years to come.

'Dog in space, oh yeah, man, no problem,' said Radius to Jack.

'Um, yeah, but what about my job?' said Stark. 'I've only got this week off to do the audition. I'm supposed to be at work next Monday.'

Fiona wrote down the details of where Stark worked.

'I mean, it's a good job,' said Stark. 'Good pension fund and everything. I wouldn't want to lose it.'

'Don't worry,' Fiona reassured him. 'I'll sort it all out.'

'Excellent,' said Radius. 'Let's go.'

He led the family through a door at the end of the room and up some stairs on to the roof of the building where a helicopter was waiting.

'And we need to talk to your grandparents too,' Radius added, just before the helicopter engine started and no-one could hear what anyone was saying.

Everything had happened so quickly. Stark Contrast – thirty-nine years old, production director for the country's biggest nut and bolt company with branches in every major city and a few in cities that were not major but seemed to use a lot of nuts and bolts – didn't like 'quickly'. He was the sort of person who liked to think about things before making a decision. Sometimes it drove his family mad.

'Oh, come on, Dad,' Primrose would say as her dad dithered at the counter of the ice-cream shop. 'Strawberry or vanilla?'

'Well, yes, but the raspberry looks nice,' Stark might reply.

'You hate raspberry,' Laura would say. 'You know you do.'

'Oh yes, so I do, I forgot,' Stark would say. 'All right then, vanilla . . . no, hang on, strawberry . . . though, if I had vanilla, I could have sprinkles . . .'

Stark had a problem with full stops. He wasn't sure they actually existed, even though he knew they really did. He just didn't know where to put them.

'Because sprinkles don't really work with strawberry, do they? And, as I always say, sprinkles add excitement to ice-cream,' he added.

This was something Stark Contrast had never said before, apart from the 'as I always say' bit, which he did all the time, even though it was never true. It was a phrase he'd inherited from his father, who had been the production director for the country's largest screw and washer company. One thing Stark's father did always say was, 'You'd be amazed at just how interesting screws and washers actually are.' Stark said the same thing about nuts and bolts and had actually invented a very special chrome molybdenum seven-and-a-half-sided nut that had been used in Patagonia's first space shuttle.[9]

In the end, Laura usually got him one scoop each of strawberry and vanilla. Before her husband

---

[9] *Which had not been a great success. It had not so much reached space as collided with an albatross and reached the bottom of the sea. The space shuttle had, however, shuttled, and fifty-seven years from now, when a salvage team will recover the wreck, Stark's special nuts will still be as shiny as the day they were made.*

could point out that they might not go very well together, she would pay and they would all walk out of the shop. And because Stark had taken so long to make up his mind, everyone else's ice-creams would've already melted and Laura would say to her husband, 'OK, darling, wait out here with Crumley, I'll go and get us all another ice-cream each.'

When it came to something big and important, it could take Stark months or even longer to make up his mind. It wasn't that he was stupid.[10] He just liked to weigh things up and consider all the options. The last time he'd bought a new family car, by the time he'd decided on one, it had become last year's model, and had been replaced by a newer and better model. Laura said that if he changed his mind again, she would go crazy, so Stark bought the one he'd been looking at. Because it was last year's model there was only one colour left, which made the decision a lot easier. And because it was last

---

[10] *'Stupid' is a very variable word. Compared to me and a lot of you, Stark Contrast was stupid. Compared to all his friends and the rest of you, he was clever.*

year's model, Stark got a fantastic discount – and bought a huge new TV with the leftover money.

'Bit of luck, that,' he said.

Except it then took him months to decide the best TV to get, by which time their old TV only worked in black and white, and, as far as Primrose was concerned, this was so embarrassing she couldn't invite any of her friends over.

So being whisked out of the queue to the top floor of a skyscraper and away to the country filled Stark's head with all sorts of questions, queries and what-ifs. He hadn't even been given time to go into work and quit his job or go down to the pub to say goodbye to all his mates.

'But . . .' he would begin – but whatever he would finish with, Fiona Hardly would say it had all been taken care of.

'Yes,' she reassured him, 'we've even organised for someone to go to your house and take care of the goldfish in the garden pond.'[11]

---

[11] *'Take care' as in 'Take care not to miss any when you take them all to the local fish and chip shop.'*

There were no 'buts' that Stark could think of that Fiona didn't have an answer for, but he was still worried.

'Listen, Fiona, my dad worries about everything,' Primrose said. 'He was even worried when a really happy bluebird landed on his shoulder and gave him a priceless diamond ring.'

Which had actually happened several months earlier on a Tuesday.

And of course, Stark had worried big time about it and taken the ring to the police station and handed it in to an embarrassingly honest policeman who gave it back to him after the specified legal time had passed.

'Then the ring obviously belongs to someone who doesn't live round here,' Stark had said.

'No, sir,' the embarrassingly honest policeman had told him. 'I have checked everywhere that isn't around here, even as far away as far and wide, and no-one has reported it missing. So the ring is one hundred per cent completely, legally and officially yours.'

When Stark still insisted it belonged to someone else, the embarrassingly honest policeman said, 'Sir, it belongs to you.'

Stark had then sold the ring and given the money to a charity that cared for really happy bluebirds that were not happy anymore and had turned grey and had lost the will to handle jewellery.[12]

Being suddenly rushed away from every single one of his comfort zones had made Stark very stressed, or rather, it would've done if he hadn't spent so long trying to decide if he was stressed or excited, so that by the time he came to a conclusion he had almost nearly sort of come to terms with the whole going-into-space thing and was beginning to think about becoming quite keen on the idea. Or not.

---

[12] *Because birds don't have hands, they can't actually 'handle' anything. They can hold things in their beaks and some can hold things in their feet too, but there is no such word as 'beakle' or 'footle,' so 'handle' will have to do.*

Comment from a very well-educated editor: 'Actually, there is such a word as footle, but it means "to waste time", so it wouldn't work in this context. And the only use for "beakle"' is as someone's surname, so that wouldn't work either. We will stick with "handle", even though no hands are involved.'

What Jack had been saying as the helicopter had taken off was, 'We haven't got any grandparents.'

'They haven't got any grandparents,' Laura had been saying too, but they were both drowned out by the helicopter.

As they flew away across the city, the massive size of the crowd surrounding the TV station became apparent. Looking at the satellite photos later, it was calculated that there were over half a million people queueing for auditions, with more still arriving and that was just at the main studios. This was repeated at the seven other LIMP-TV studios around the world.

'Did you say something?' Radius said when

they'd finally landed and were walking up the lawn towards the mansion.

'Yes,' said Jack. 'I said we haven't got any grandparents.'

'It's true,' Laura said. 'Stark and I are both orphans. Saint Prunella's Home for Unwanted Orphans – that's where we met.'

'How touching,' Radius's mouth said while his brain thought, *DAMN, DAMN, DAMN!!*

But then, he said to himself, *I haven't got where I am today without turning every setback into an opportunity.*

'We'll find you one,' he said.

'Find us one? One what?' said Laura.

'A parent,' said Radius. 'One will do.'

'We've tried,' said Laura. 'We've searched through every record we could lay our hands on, but neither of us could find the slightest trace of any of our ancestors.'

'Don't worry, dear lady,' said Radius. 'We'll get you one.'

'But, they won't be our real grandparent,' said Primrose.

'Yes, they will,' Fiona Hardly said. 'Sure, they won't be your own personal one, but they'll probably be someone else's grandparent. I mean, most old people are.'

'But we might not like them and they might not like us.'

'Yes, they will,' said Radius. 'The granny will love you.'

What he meant was, he would pay some old actress a lot of money to pretend to love them even if she didn't, and because she would be quite a good actress and everyone wants to believe it when someone tells them that they love them, the Contrasts would believe it.

It was all beginning to take shape.

Once again, Radius had turned the potential disaster of no grandparents into an added benefit. Instead of some old lady who could possibly leak all over the spaceship, talk to imaginary people in the wallpaper and, perish the thought, even have a mind of her own, he would have an insider who would do whatever he told her to and the family wouldn't

even suspect it. He decided one old person would be enough. There was no point in wasting money and besides, two old people together could cause all sorts of problems, and there was only one type of problem Radius Limpfast liked and that was a problem he was totally in control of.

I'm so good at this, he said to himself. *Maybe I should've used actors for all of it and a scriptwriter and . . . Oh no, that's called drama, isn't it? I haven't got where I am today by wasting money on scriptwriters and professional actors, and I'm not going to start now.*

He's so good at this, Fiona Hardly said to herself.

She realised straight away that the granny was going to be an actress and so if things got a bit boring, she could be used to spice things up. Of course, Radius had secret plans far bigger than anyone could have guessed, not even Fiona, who seemed to be able to read her boss's mind.

In fact, it was probably not that she could read his mind, but that she had a head full of devious ideas that matched his exactly – except that Radius had more levels of deviousness and they went far deeper

than hers. He had known, right from the start, that being stuck inside a glass bubble on a dead rock did not have a lot going for it in the action department. He knew it would only be a matter of time, and probably quite a short time too, before the family began getting bored, but that didn't matter, because Radius Limpfast had a Plan B.

He also had Plans C, D, E, F, G, H right down to Plan Z and beyond, but they were all locked away in his head with coded copies hidden safely away in his top-secret safe. In fact, he had a whole second and third alphabet full of plans to keep *Watch This Space* running for years, and he had no doubt at all that more and more brilliant ideas would come to him in his sleep as time went by.

So, he said to himself, *it's all good.*[13] *And, if I'm not mistaken*, he added, *my brilliant assistant will probably come up with a few great ideas of her own.*

'By the way, RR,' Fiona said when they were out of anyone else's earshot, 'perhaps you could get

---

[13] *Meaning, 'In a way that made lots of money without having to bother with all those stupid things like morals and honesty.'*

Professor to implant a secret two-way radio in the grandmother's head, so you can have direct contact with her whenever you want.'

'Brilliant!' said Radius.

Behind them, the helicopter flew back to the city to collect Crumley, leaving them alone in the middle of nowhere. Apart from the big mansion, Limpfast Manor, there were no other signs of human life – no roads, no buildings, no man-made sounds, just an endless countryside of woods, occasional fields of lush green grass dotted with lakes and rivers and a few cows and horses.

There had been a road to the house in the old days, but when Radius had bought the place and the surrounding area, he had had the roads ripped out and replaced with grass and trees. There had been several villages and farms with houses, but they were gone now. And, of course, there was no-one left to ask where they'd all gone, which was a good thing.

Now the only way to reach Limpfast Manor was by helicopter, or by walking, which was inadvisable due to the booby traps, pits full of spiky sticks,

lions, mountains of lion poo and bombs that ringed the entire estate. There was also, as a final security measure, the special Bio-Dynamic Barbed Wire.[14] A few people had tried – mostly the sort of people who wore big baggy shorts and rucksacks full of thermos flasks of cold tea – and bits of them were stuck in the tree branches, where they had either been blown or stashed away by the lions.

'Well, people, welcome to my home,' said Radius, as they went through the front door of Limpfast Manor, into the massive entrance hall. 'Relax, settle in, enjoy. Anything you want, just ask one of my staff.'

---

[14] *An invention of Radius's of which he was particularly proud. It was a special barbed wire that reached out and grabbed people if they went too near it and then, in the space of a few hours, dissolved them, leaving no trace they had ever existed. It had proved invaluable in several series of reality shows Radius had created where the contestants – or 'idiots', as Radius liked to call them – were taken out into the middle of nowhere to try to win a lot of very dangerous games. Naturally, some of the less stupid idiots always tried to run away, which is where the Bio-Dynamic Barbed Wire came in so handy.*

The Contrasts were taken upstairs and shown to their rooms. They were each told that dinner would be at seven-thirty and were handed a map that would lead them back to one of the staircases to the dining room.

It was all just so incredible. Only a few hours ago, the Contrasts had been one of the hundreds of thousands of families queueing up in the grey city streets around the world, and now they were in another world – one full of excitement and unknown possibilities and the promise of fame and fortune. (Their fame would be massive, but it wouldn't be until quite a bit later that they'd realise the fortune part had never actually been mentioned.)

'Isn't this brilliant?' said Jack to Primrose when he finally found her room. 'My bed's nearly as big as my whole bedroom at home.'

'Yeah, yeah,' said Primrose, 'but there's no phone signal here. I mean, I can't tell ANYONE! It's dreadful. Like, all my Facebook friends will think I'm dead.'

The phone signal thing wasn't exactly true – there was just no signal for any of the Contrasts' phones. There was no way Radius wanted any of them, especially the daughter-with-attitude, ringing their friends or the newspapers or anyone else in the outside world. From now on, every single word the Contrasts said and, hopefully, thought would be carefully controlled.

But in a thoughtful, caring sort of way, Radius said to himself.[15]

---

[15] *'Thoughtful' because Radius had thought of it, and 'caring' because he didn't care if they did find out, as by then there would be nothing they could do about it.*

Introducing LAURA CONTRAST

Laura Contrast had no problem making her mind up about anything. She didn't waste time filling her head with questions. There were too many other things for her to fill, like all the drawers and shelves in her walk-in wardrobe, her social diary, the family bank account and the heads of her husband and children.[16] There were no should-I-get-the-red-shoes-or-the-black-ones problems in her life. She just bought both pairs, and quite often got fed up with them before she'd even reached home.

Every month Laura was voted Donator of the Month at four out of the five charity shops in their suburb. The fifth charity shop specialised in nylon and Laura did her best to be a nylon-free zone.

The first time she had seen Stark at the International Nut and Bolt Expo, she had decided that he would become her husband. She had never had a problem with that sort of thing. She was very attractive and men, boys, even small dogs

---

[16] *She had given up trying to control the dog's mind. He seemed immune to her charms and was totally devoted to Stark.*

loved her. They all fell adoringly at her feet, happy to follow her blindly around like puppies.[17]

Stark Contrast was good-looking, but not so good-looking that all her friends would be after him. He was just the right height to see over the top of her head, which could be useful when shopping, but not so tall that he could look down on her. He had an important, safe, reliable job in one of the biggest nut and bolt companies in the world and, to top it off, he was the inventor of the legendary, nay, almost mythical, chrome molybdenum seven-and-a-half-sided nut.

Two days after the Expo finished, she and Stark were engaged and what seemed like only fifteen minutes later – but was actually seventeen thousand, two hundred and eighty minutes – they were married.

---

[17] *She had been there as a rookie journalist. The newspaper she was working for made a habit of sending out their new recruits to the most boring assignments they could find. If the recruit could actually write an article that made the assignment interesting, they were kept on. If not, they'd have to leave at the end of the month. Laura had stayed for several years.*

Laura had ticked marriage off her mental list, moved on to the next things on the list and, approximately half a million minutes later, Primrose had been born. A lot more minutes later, Jack had followed. So that was the first three things on her clipboard completed exactly as planned. Laura assumed that the fourth and final thing on her list would automatically follow and, by and large, it did, though her daughter could be a bit of a handful from time to time. The fourth thing was, 'Live happily ever after'.

It had been Laura who had suggested the family apply to be in the TV show. The idea of being incredibly famous appealed to her, especially because, as far as she could tell, she wouldn't actually have to do that much. The kids were as keen as she was, but by the time Laura had downloaded the application form, filled it out, added her husband's credit card details and sent it off, Stark was still saying that they should probably think about it and weigh up all the pros and cons.

'Yes, well, you do that,' Laura had said, 'and then you'll be ready to apply for the third series.'

She had even already bought clothes for the family to wear to the audition. Once again, Stark had said he needed to think about that, because he couldn't really see what was wrong with the reindeer cardigan his mum had knitted for him, which he always wore on special occasions.

'People like my cardigan,' he'd said. 'It makes them feel relaxed.'

'No, darling, it makes them feel well dressed,' Laura had replied.

Now, Laura assumed it was her excellent taste in audition clothes that had caused them to be chosen. Her only regret was that they had been whisked off to the mansion so fast that she'd had no time to pack, which was both a bad thing and a good thing. It was a bad thing because she only had the clothes she was wearing and by mid-afternoon, which it currently was, she would usually have changed clothes at least twice since getting up that morning. But then it was a good thing because it

meant she would usually have to go online and buy new clothes.

Except there was no internet.

rRego's Inventions*

The High-Tension Long-Reach Safety Tethering System, stupid humans for the retrieving of.

* Just be patient, you'll meet rRego later.

For the next five days the Contrasts felt like they were living in a luxury resort. It was as if they had died and gone to heaven. There was nothing any of them could think of that wasn't there.

'Apart from the internet,' said Primrose. 'And, like, my mobile and Facebook.'

'And the fact that I've got nothing to wear,' said Laura, who was not naked so obviously did have something to wear.

'I'm sorry about that,' Radius lied. 'Some satellite problem, apparently. I've got my guys working on it.'

'Isn't there, like, somewhere in the village where I could go online?' said Primrose.

'Yes, I'll go too,' Laura agreed. 'I need to buy some clothes.'

'Village, what village?' said Radius.

'Well, there must be a village or another house or something.'

'No, not near enough to walk to.'

'Yeah, well, so why can't we drive there?' Primrose went on and on and on and on.

Radius was getting impatient.

'I'm sure we can sort something out,' said Fiona, seeing her boss was close to losing it. 'Just give me a couple of hours and I'll see what I can do.'

The 'what I can do' involved one of the communications technicians, Bill – who lived full-time at Limpfast Manor, making sure that Radius always had faultless super-fast connections to every bit of his media empire – and one of the kitchen staff, Beryl.

'What I need you to do, Bill,' Fiona explained, 'is to set up a self-contained internet so that the wretched Contrast daughter can go online without being online. I need her to think she has contact with

57

the outside world when in fact she is in contact with you, Beryl, while you're in one of the soundproof recording rooms in the basement.'

So Bill the technician created an entire fake internet.[18] It looked just like the real internet, but it was all inside one small computer two floors down from where Primrose would be.

'Well, there's good news and there's bad news,' said Fiona, when she went back to Primrose's room. 'I've got you some internet, but I'm afraid the phone lines, mobiles and landlines are still out of order. I've phoned the telephone company. Er, no, I mean, I've emailed the telephone company, but all they said was that they were working on it.'

Then she added, 'But please don't tell anyone where you are or that you're going to the moon.'

'OK, OK, I won't,' snapped Primrose.

And she didn't.

---

[18] *This wasn't as complicated as it sounds, because Radius had several fake internets at Limpfast Manor for when important people, who might have useful information or secrets, came to stay.*

Not.

Of course the first thing Primrose did was email her best friend, Nazzy, and tell her that she was going to the moon.

It took quite a while for Primrose to get through. She typed in Nazzy's email address, then Bill emailed the same address pretending to be Primrose, but just said they were on holiday, not that they were about to go to the moon. Nazzy emailed back, and then Beryl replied to Primrose, pretending to be Nazzy. If Nazzy's email message was harmless, Beryl just cut and pasted it into the fake reply. If the email had stuff that might be a bit awkward, then Beryl sent something different which of course was totally confusing to everyone except Primrose, who thought it was all real or as real as her internet life was, especially the site with all the kitten photos.

After about an hour, everyone was getting really fed up with the whole thing, so Fiona slid her hand across her throat and Bill pulled the plug.

Primrose was suspicious.

Her friend, Nazzy, had been really weird. Nazzy was always weird, but it was different this time. She kept using strange words that Primrose had never heard her use before and she didn't seem the slightest bit excited about the moon stuff, which was really weird because Nazzy got excited about everything, even something as pathetic as a photo of a kitten.

It was almost like she was a different person, Primrose thought, *but then she's probably freaking out that I'm actually going to the moon. Can't wait until she tells everyone at school. They'll be so jealous.*

Laura was a lot easier to sort out. She and Fiona were about the same size and shape and they both liked similar clothes, so Fiona just let Laura choose some of hers. When Laura saw the expensive names on the labels, she was only too happy to do so.

'It's just until we get the internet back on,' she said.

'Of course,' Fiona agreed. 'And once you're on your way to the moon, you'll all be wearing special spacesuits anyway.'

'Spacesuits?' said Laura.

'Don't worry,' Fiona said quickly. 'They are very elegant. I supervised the designs myself.'

'Colour?' said Laura.

'Yes, loads of it,' Fiona said. 'After all, they're probably going to be the clothes that will be seen by the most people in the whole world at the same time ever, even more than Lady Diana's crumply wedding dress. You will look amazing.'

Naturally, most of this was rubbish. There was no way Radius Limpfast was going to spend that sort of money to get cool designer spacesuits made, and even if he did, they would still have LIMP-TV printed all over them in bright neon lettering. Which they did – all over the silver nylon fronts, sleeves, legs and backs, so that no matter which angle the Contrasts were viewed from, the writing was big, bold and impossible to miss.

Meanwhile, Stark and Jack believed everything they were told. Radius Limpfast reckoned that was pretty good – a family of four with half of them totally trusting him. Fifty-fifty was the standard odds on which he had built his success.

61

'I mean,' he said to Fiona Hardly, 'we could reject the Contrasts and look for a family that was one hundred per cent gullible, but I reckon this family will give us more opportunities. Because, as we both know, living in a glass box on a barren rock covered in dust doesn't have a lot going for it. So we need all the help we can get, and I reckon the Contrasts will work perfectly.'

'Not to mention the apparently helpful robot they'll have with them,' said Fiona. 'And the sweet little old granny we'll be giving them.'

'Yes, indeed,' Radius agreed. 'We must get the granny organised.'

This one goes forwards in time.

rREGO's*

AMAZING

TIME

MACHINE

And this one goes backwards.

* You will meet rRego soon.

Introducing PRIMROSE CONTRAST and JACK CONTRAST

Primrose Contrast was fourteen going on five or twenty-six, depending on what mood she was in. She was not fat like most of the girls at school, and although she had angry hair she was quite pretty, but not as pretty as her mother. Whatever age Primrose was being, she knew her family were idiots. She was so much cleverer than they were in every single way. In fact, quite often, she didn't believe that Stark and Laura Contrast were her real parents.

'I reckon I'm adopted,' she had said to her friend, Nazzy. 'My real dad is probably some brilliant genius scientist and my mum is, like, a famous movie star.'

'That is, like, so weird,' said Nazzy, 'because I reckon I'm adopted too. I mean, my mum and dad are total bucketheads. My real dad is probably, like, some computer genius billionaire and my mum's a famous movie star too.'

'Hey, maybe our real mums know each other,' said Primrose, but at the same time she was thinking, *Yeah right, as if your parents would be anyone brilliant. You're as big a buckethead as they are.*

And Nazzy, real name Anastasia, was actually Primrose's best friend. She was also Primrose's least best friend because she was Primrose's only friend due to Primrose thinking all the other girls she knew were either nerds or spotty or stupid or ugly, or all four.

As for boys, Primrose thought every one she met was either a nerd or spotty or stupid or ugly or all four, except for Harold, who was quite good-looking, incredibly intelligent and not in the slightest bit interested in her, even though she'd given him a Vegemite sandwich when he'd lost his lunch on the bus. He hadn't so much lost it on the bus as *under* the bus, when the bus arrived and ran the sandwich over.

Primrose actually liked quite a lot of boys, but they were in magazines and not real life.

Even if her mum and dad were her real parents, there was no way her thicko brother Jack was her real brother. He was definitely adopted.

'Mum and Dad aren't your real mum and dad,' she kept telling him. 'They found you in a ditch. Mum told me. When they took you to the police, the police said you were so ugly and stupid that

no-one would want you, and that Mum and Dad had to keep you.'

Then Jack would burst into tears and run to tell Laura, who would shout at Primrose and send her to her room, but Primrose thought it was worth it, especially as it meant she wouldn't be sent outside to get some sunshine and fresh air and all that boring nature stuff.

Jack Contrast was one year younger than Primrose and had almost nothing in common with her. For a start, he was a boy. He had spots and his sister didn't, apart from a rather painful one she had in a secret place so embarrassing that even she had never looked at it. Jack always smelled of boiled cabbage, even though he had never eaten it.[19] Primrose smelled of

---

[19] *Jack had smelled like this ever since birth, and it was enough to put his parents off cabbage forever, so no-one in the family ever ate it. Smelling of cabbage is a recognised disease called Smelling of Cabbage Syndrome or Stinky Boy,*

Roses – not the ones growing in the garden but the chocolates that come in a box.

Jack only seemed to have one hobby and that was picking his spots, at which he was an expert. Once he managed to keep a spot on his forehead going for over a year, by picking the scab off at exactly the right time.

Jack did have a second hobby, though most people just thought there was something wrong with him. He was a farter of Olympic standard, capable of letting them out exactly when he wanted to, and with a choice of six different flavours, all of which were revolting.

Jack did not have a lot going for him, though his farting talent had made him a lot of friends at school – strange friends, admittedly, who were spottier and smellier than he was.

---

because it only happens to boys, especially ones who never eat cabbage. So far it has never occurred to anyone that eating cabbage might actually cure the disease – which it does.

eanwhile, at the top-secret production facility hidden deep in Tristan da Cunha/Patagonia/Wales/Belgium/Poland,[20] work on the MUD (Moon Unit Dwelling) was progressing according to Radius's instructions.

'This isn't a construction that we're going to use over and over again,' Radius explained to the builders, 'so you don't need to use strong materials, like thick sheets of titanium. Thin aluminium will do, with fibreglass and gaffer tape. You could even use flattened tin cans here and there for some of the smaller bits, but make sure you take the labels

---

[20] *It is so secret that even I don't know where it is and have just put down a shortlist of what I think are the most likely places. It may well be none of them because they all seem too likely.*

off first. I mean, we don't want baked-bean labels drifting around the moon.'

'Right, boss,' said the foreman.

'That was a joke,' said Radius. 'The bit about the tin cans.'

'Oh. Haha, boss, great joke!'

'Though, actually, flattened tin cans are pretty strong,' said the designer. 'We could use them in quite a few places where there isn't any stress on the framework.'

'Oh. Haha, great joke!' said the rest of the construction team.

'I wasn't joking,' said the designer. 'We could save thousands.'

'Brilliant,' said Radius. 'That's my kind of thinking. But do remember to take the labels off.'

Radius told them all that every cost-saving measure they could come up with would earn them a bonus. This, of course, meant that there was some serious cost saving – though the designer did draw the line at using toilet-roll tubes. So the builders went online and bought:

1. *Several garden sheds = bedrooms*
2. *Lots of clear plastic sheeting = living areas and bits to join the sheds together*
3. *Buckets = kitchen*
4. *Different buckets = lavatories*
5. *Mops and different, different buckets = see point 3 and especially point 4*
6. *Gaffer tape = join everything together*
7. *Other stuff*

There were some things they had to buy from proper Outer Space Colony Suppliers, like lunar panels,[21] oxygen tanks, water tanks, food, bandaids and a nuclear fusion bacon generator.[22]

After the whole thing had been covered in several layers of cooking foil, the MUD looked pretty good, unless you were actually considering living in it in zero-gravity conditions with zero oxygen or unless you looked at it from closer than five metres

---

[21] *Which are like solar panels, but with lots of bricks tied to them to stop them from floating away in zero gravity. They also bought lunar underpants, which are like Earth underpants but also fitted with anti-gravity bricks.*

[22] *I actually have one of these. It can make bacon out of thin air, though it's not as good as bacon made out of fat pigs.*

away. But Radius had thought of that and had already ordered some special rose-coloured romantic soft-focus camera lenses for the outside shots of the building. He also had several small MUD models in a 'genuine' moon landscape set on a small table in one of the cellars under Limpfast Manor for filming long shots.

'It will look brilliant,' he told Fiona, who agreed.

'It looks brilliant,' he told the Contrasts, when he showed them the photos.

The family were impressed, apart from Primrose, who said, 'It looks like a little model.'

'So do you, dear,' said Radius.

The people in the casting office at LIMP-TV headquarters, who usually selected the actors and actresses lovingly called 'contestants' for the reality TV shows, had gone through the files and made a shortlist of six possible grannies. So while the Contrasts went through a course of fitness training in the woods that surrounded Limpfast Manor, Radius and Fiona flew back to the city to audition the grannies.

The fitness training wasn't exactly hard work. Fiona had told the family they would be doing Pilates, which is a strangely popular exercise regime for yuppies. The Contrasts had heard of it, but hadn't the faintest idea what it was. So they were delighted to discover that Fiona Hardly's version was

actually called 'Pielattes' and involved eating meat pies and drinking cafe lattes at three-hourly intervals throughout the day and doing a bit of running around and jumping up and down in between.

'Though, of course,' Fiona explained, 'once you get to the moon, you won't be able to do either of these things or else you will float off into space. You could try doing them inside the MUD with the gravity unit turned on, but it's quite small so you'd probably keep hitting your heads.'

Fiona did not tell them that, because of the rather small old-technology solar panels on the MUD, the gravity unit would only be turned on at meal times and when they were doing their 'live broadcasts'[23] to Earth. Nor did she tell the Contrasts that every minute of every day when they were not doing their 'live broadcasts', they would be secretly filmed in every part of the MUD except for the

---

[23] *The meaning of 'live' in this case actually meant, 'No way is this going to be live. No-one is allowed to see anything until we have gone through it and edited out all the bits we don't like.'*

lavatories. That was one thing Radius had not been happy about.

'I mean,' he'd objected, 'just think of the hilarious material we'd get. One of them sits down on the toilet and just as they do a poo we turn off the gravity unit.'

'Gross,' said the designers.

'Totally,' Radius agreed. 'Great, isn't it?'

The designers, who had early on realised the only way to get Radius to agree to something was to tell him it would save him money, said that poo floating around inside the MUD would get into the equipment and probably wreck it. So Radius reluctantly agreed to no cameras in the toilets and automatic gravity when anyone used them.

'It's a hell of a wasted opportunity, though,' he said.

'Yes,' said the designers, 'but it's saving you money.'

'I don't see how,' said Radius.

'All the poo and stuff will go into a methane generator and produce free electricity,' the designers explained.

Being told it would save money cheered Radius up, though he still wished he could have played around with the toilets.

None of the six shortlisted grannies were what Radius had in mind.

'Are you sure there weren't others who might be better?' he asked the casting office.

'No,' they said. 'There were lots who were great in some ways but completely wrong in others, and there were dozens who were just too old.'

'We want old,' said Radius.

'Yes, we know that, but I'm sure you want them to live long enough to make it to the moon and that you want them to have all their marbles. We had two who seemed perfect on paper, but then they died in the waiting room while we were doing the interviews.'

'Fair enough.'

'And dying on TV is not a big crowd-pleaser,'

said the casting people. 'Remember what happened with the cobra juggler on *So You Think You've Still Got Your Marbles*?'

'Oh, yes, bit embarrassing, that,' said Radius. 'Not to mention the payout we had to make to the family.'

There was a clattering and a crash outside the door followed by quite a lot of superb, top-quality swearing. The door opened and a tea trolley came in, pushed by an old lady.

'Sorry about that,' she said. 'Trolley crashed into a small boy. I mean, who leaves a small boy lying around in a TV station? No adult anywhere looking after him.'

'You mean he was lying on the floor?' said Radius.

'Well, he was after the trolley ran into him,' the tea lady explained.

One of the casting staff went to the door.

'Where are you going?' Radius asked her.

'I'm going to see if the child is all right,' she explained.

77

'Oh, don't worry about that,' Radius said. 'The cleaners will clear him away. No, no, sit down, this is far more important.'

'But . . .' the casting lady began.

'Come on, sit down,' Radius said and turned to the tea lady. 'So, have you ever been on TV?'

'Don't be silly, dear,' said the tea lady. 'I'm a tea lady, not an actress. Mind you, it doesn't look that difficult. But look at me, I'm an old lady.'

'You are indeed,' Radius agreed. 'And an old lady is exactly what we are looking for.'

'What are you talking about, you silly man?' said the tea lady, completely unaware of who Radius was. 'Here, have a cup of tea and a biscuit.'

Radius told her who he was and was quite upset when she didn't seem in the slightest bit impressed, but not as upset as he normally would've been because he knew that the tea lady was exactly what he was looking for. He told her why he thought that she'd be the perfect granny.

'Perfect? It's a long time since anyone's called me that,' she said. 'Go to the moon, you say?'

'Yes,' said Radius. 'What do you reckon? You haven't got any chocolate digestives, have you?'

'Chocolate digestives? They're only allowed for the top executives, but then, that's you, isn't it? Here.'

'Thank you,' said Radius. 'So what about it then?'

'What about what?'

'Going to the moon,' said Radius. 'What do you reckon?'

'I'd need to get my hair done first,' said the tea lady. 'You'd have to pay for that. I can't afford it on my wages.'

A quick phone call to the wages department made Radius go white with shock and then red with embarrassment.

'I will pay you exactly one hundred times what you are earning now,' he said. 'And on top of that, you will become the world's most famous granny.'

Then he explained exactly what was involved. He told her about the Contrasts, who they were and where they were and how they had no granny of their own.

'You mean, the winning family has been chosen?' said the tea lady. 'What are all those crowds doing out there, then?'

'Well, we haven't actually told anyone about the Contrasts,' Radius explained. 'You're the first person outside the family to know about it. Oh, by the way, what's your name?'

'Apricot,' said Apricot.

'Apricot? That's a strange name.'

'My dad sold fruit, and apricots were his favourite,' Apricot explained.

'It may bit a bit unusual, but I like it,' said Radius. 'Granny Apricot – it's got a good ring to it.'

'Do you, er, like children?' the chief casting executive asked.

'Dunno,' said Apricot. 'I've never actually had any.'

'And is there a Mister Apricot?'

'No, dear, never had one of those, either. It wasn't that I didn't want to. It was just that I never found one I wanted to keep,' said Apricot.

'So, no family at all?' the Radius asked.

Apricot shook her head.

'Not even a distant cousin or nephew three times removed?' said Fiona.

'No.'

Brilliant, Radius thought. *That'll save a bit on the insurance.*

While Radius sat in his office working out the best way to tell the world that the family had been chosen in a way that wouldn't cause riots, Fiona took Granny Apricot out to get her hair done and to buy her some new clothes.

'Mind you,' Radius said to no-one in particular when he had come to the conclusion that there was no way to present the Contrasts to everyone without causing any anger, 'it could make us a few dollars.'

He rang his program planners.

'New reality show,' he said. 'Production will start on Monday. Series title: *So You Think You Can Riot.*'

'What?' said the planners at first.

'Wow, brilliant!' they said when Radius explained it to them.

On the other hand, Radius said to himself, *we've got so many people tied up with* Watch This Space, *we'd have to take on a whole lot of new staff, and not only that, a riot series could distract people from our main thing.*

He was, as usual, absolutely right. Research had shown that ninety per cent of LIMP-TV's viewers couldn't concentrate on more than one thing at a time, and in fact sixty-four per cent couldn't concentrate on one thing for more than fourteen minutes without needing a bag of chips.

So he came up with fairly simple solution. LIMP-TV announced:

BRILLIANT NEWS!!

BECAUSE OF THE WORLD-SHATTERING RESPONSE WE HAVE HAD FROM YOU, OUR WONDERFUL, WONDERFUL, BRILLIANT VIEWERS, WE HAVE DECIDED THAT WE ARE GOING TO

HAVE A SECOND AND A THIRD ROUND,
AND MAYBE TEN MORE ROUNDS
OF AUDITIONS. SO IF YOU DIDN'T
MAKE IT THE PREVIOUS TIME, YOU
CAN APPLY FOR FREE AND KEEP ON
APPLYING FOR FREE TO ALL OF THEM.
GO HOME NOW AND STAY TUNED FOR
THE ANNOUNCEMENT OF THE NEXT
AUDITIONS.

'And, of course, by then our family will be up
on the moon and everyone will forget about any
auditions,' Radius explained. 'They'll all be totally
focused on the Contrasts.'

'Brilliant,' said Fiona and everyone else.

Meanwhile, at another top-secret production facility hidden deep in Tristan da Cunha/Patagonia/ the Australian Outback/Belgium/Poland,[24] work was being done on the BUMPS (Bionic Ultrafast Moon People Spaceship) and the huge cargo rocket that would take the MUD to the moon.

Even the chief engineer – José MacO'Learolski, who was one of Radius's top engineers – did not know where any of the top-secret locations were, even though he was in charge of the MUD and the BUMPS. He controlled and coordinated everything from a small top-secret cave high up on Mount Everest/K2/Kangchenjunga/Lhotse/

---

[24] *See footnote 20.*

Mount Bongo[25] and was connected to the two top-secret production facilities by a closed-circuit super top-secret internet.

It wasn't just that Radius was extremely suspicious of spies from the press and especially other TV networks leaking pictures of the MUD and of the BUMPS, it was also that he did not want anyone finding out about his 'cost-effective measures'.

So if a few of the MUD's seals were filled with porridge instead of high-grade silicone sealant, all it would mean is that a tiny-weeny bit of the Contrasts' air supply might leak out. It wouldn't be a problem and if it was, well, hey, that'd make for great television and there was plenty more porridge in the larder unit.

'And the family all seem very fit and healthy, so holding their breath for a bit while the robot fixes the leak won't be a problem,' Radius explained to José.

What Radius didn't know was that the mechanic who was fitting the seals loved porridge

---

[25] *See footnote 24.*

more than any other food, so some of the porridge used to seal the MUD's windows was second-hand.[26]

There were many other corner-cutting procedures. In fact, by the end, neither the BUMPS nor MUD had a single corner anywhere. They had all been cut, though Radius had not been as tight with the costs of the BUMPS as he had been with the MUD because it would have looked very bad if the Contrasts had died or exploded or crashed into the sea, a mountain, a tall building or the sun before they had landed safely on the moon. Also, he had reluctantly agreed with the designers that the spaceship should be able to bring the family safely back to Earth at the end of the series.

Though coming back to Earth in a dramatic fireball would probably get the highest viewing figures ever and break all times-viewed figures on YouTube, he thought to himself.

---

[26] *Probably best if you don't think about that.*

Fiona and Granny Apricot were going to spend the morning shopping, with the emphasis on the 'spend' bit.

It was one of those incredibly rare moments when Radius was prepared to spend big. And rare as those moments were, this one was even rarer. It was unique,[27] because Radius handed the credit card to Fiona. Letting someone else use one of his no-cash-limit credit cards was probably the most

---

[27] *This would be a good time for you to learn the REAL meaning of the word 'unique'. Things CANNOT be 'a bit unique' or 'very unique' or even 'totally unique'. They can only be 'unique', because it means 'one of a kind' and NOT 'one of several'. Unique means unique.*

significant thing Radius had done since he had sold his grandmother to a research laboratory.[28]

While Fiona stood with her back to him, watching every tiny move he made in the magnifying hinges of her glasses,[29] Radius Limpfast opened the top-secret triple-locked safe hidden behind a painting of his mother,[30] which hung on the wall behind his chair in his top-top-top executive office. Inside the safe was a safe, and inside that safe were some credit cards, a ridiculously massive diamond and an even more ridiculously massive gold nugget.

Radius took one of the credit cards out of the safe and wiped the dust off it before locking both

---

[28] *Though he'd got his grandmother back, eventually – in fifteen jam jars.*

[29] *Fiona had spent years practising with her special glasses until she could not only see the tiniest detail, like a PIN, in their hinges, but she could also remember every single one of the tiniest details she had seen.*

[30] *Radius himself had painted the picture of his mother when he had been eight years old. It was dreadful and made her look like a lumpy goldfish, when she actually looked like quite a smooth haddock.*

safes again and sliding his mother's portrait back into place.

As she took the card, Fiona realised the massive significance of the situation and her eyes almost but not quite filled with tears. Her mouth opened, but no words came out. Radius's mouth opened too and a very small scared whimper came out.

They both wanted to rush into each other's arms, but this is not that kind of book, so they didn't.[31]

Radius told Fiona to spare no expense in buying stuff for Granny Apricot. The old lady was like the kind granny he'd never had, as opposed to the nasty one he'd sold off.

'We don't want her to look like she's rich,' he said. 'Just fit her out so she looks like she's from those nauseating fifties American family TV series where everyone goes to Granny for reassurance and to eat her lovely apple pie, and she sorts out all their problems with sickly sweet advice and they live

---

[31] *Yet. So, to use the name of a very famous TV show, watch this space.*

89

happily ever after. You know, nice cardigan, eau de Cologne and hair like the Queen Mother's. We want the Contrasts to fall in love with her.'

Fiona felt her beating heart calm down as she slipped the credit card in her pocket. 'No problem, RR,' she said.

'Of course, we both know that old Apricot swears like a trooper and couldn't be further from a sweet old TV granny if she tried,' Radius added. 'But hey, great ratings when all that comes out!'

'Too right.'

As Fiona took Granny Apricot down to the ground floor in the lift, she found herself thinking about ancient relatives and wondering if the rumours about Radius selling his grandmother to a research laboratory were true and, if they were, was it the same research laboratory she'd sent her doddery grandfather to? The fact that Radius had actually got paid for his grandmother was really impressive. All she'd got for hers was a receipt and a cup of tea.

'We want to make you look nice and homely,' she told Granny Apricot, as they stood in a sea

90

of cardigans and twin-sets in the senior citizens department of the biggest and best store in town.

'Do I have to?' said Granny Apricot. 'I've spent my whole life avoiding cardigans and face powder and big beige knickers. There was a time when I used to creep up behind old ladies who dressed like that and set fire to them.'

'Oh, was that you?' said Fiona. 'I remember that. It was all over the news a few years ago. From what I know, they never found out who did it. They kept arresting teenage kids, but they couldn't find the real culprit.'

'That's right, dear,' said Apricot. 'After all, who would suspect a little old lady?'

'It was a miracle no-one was killed,' said Fiona.

'Well, I only used matches,' Apricot explained. 'I didn't use petrol or anything like that, so the fire was bound to go out before it proved fatal.'

'Some of those nylon things can go up in a flash.'

'Oh, I know,' said Apricot, 'and that's why I only set fire to pure wool. And to make sure no-one

would die, I always sniffed them out first – if they smelled of wee, I knew they'd be too damp to burn badly.'[32]

'You are so wicked,' Fiona said, laughing.

'I know, but it was such fun.'

'You are going to be the perfect granny for our show,' said Fiona.

She explained that Apricot would have a secret two-way radio to keep in touch with her and Radius, and that although the TV program itself would be live around the whole world, the cameras, which would be everywhere, would be filming twenty-four seven.

'We want you to keep your eyes open for any opportunity to make things more interesting and exciting. Dangerous is fine, but not life-threatening. You'll have one ally up there – the robot. He'll help you.'

'OK,' said Granny Apricot.

Because all this was so far away from being a tea lady, it took a bit of getting used to. In fact, Granny

---

[32] *I have been told to say, Don't try this at home.*

Apricot decided that she would probably never get used to it. The Fiona lady seemed OK, but her boss was another story. Apricot could tell that he would be totally unscrupulous. Radius Limpfast was famous for being a mercenary, an arrogant dictator with no conscience at all. But the thing was, everyone loved his TV programs. They were incredibly addictive. So if the occasional contestant got slightly broken or dead, they could overlook it. There would always be a perfectly good explanation, which everyone was only too happy to believe.

So Apricot figured that as long as she was getting her new, very large monthly pay cheque, she was going to go along with whatever they wanted. And if that didn't work out, well, hey, she'd got a lot of new clothes out of it – some she actually liked and some that would fetch a good price on eBay.

At the end of the afternoon, Fiona bought some big luxury suitcases, in which she packed all of Granny Apricot's shopping, and together they took a taxi to Apricot's house, where they collected a few things and turned off the gas. They drove back

to the TV station and boarded the helicopter, which took them down to the country to meet Apricot's new 'family' – the Contrasts.

rRego's Inventions

The Radio-Controlled
Homing Dog Bone.
Please note: by covering
the bone with chocolate,
the bone can also be used
to retrieve small boys.

Introducing CRUMLEY the dog

Crumley the dog came from a long line of feral mongrels. His mother and father and their parents before them had all been mongrels and had been so for more generations than anyone could discover. When the Contrasts had rescued him from the animal shelter as a puppy, his paperwork said he was a labradoodanielterrierhound cross, which was a pretentious, dishonest word for a mongrel.

Crumley looked a bit like a spaniel that had been dragged backwards through a hedge, fallen into a muddy puddle and crossed with a giant furball. It was impossible to tell where his actual body ended and his fur began. Sometimes it was difficult to tell exactly where his eyes were, and his tail, which never stopped wagging with pure happiness, was a permanent blur.

I are a mongrel, Crumley said to himself, *and proud of it. I will eat poo and I will pee up old people's legs. I are a happy boy.*

And Crumley was happy. He loved his family and they loved him. He had more than three red rubber balls, a comfy bed in every room and there were no cats about.

And wherever he went, as long as some of his humans were there, he thought it was the best place in the world and wanted to be nowhere else.

With one exception: the bathtub.

Stark had tried to give him a bath once. He had coaxed Crumley upstairs and into the bathroom and had shut the door before the poor dog realised what was supposed to happen next. Stark picked Crumley up and lowered him into the bathtub, which was full of nice, warm soapy water.

As if by magic, Crumley instantly became about ten times bigger and grew six more legs. At least, it seemed that way. The bathtub was much too small for Crumley and all the water to fit in at the same time. Lots of water leapt out, and then Crumley did too. Even though the door was shut, the water managed to escape.

'Who knew there were so many gaps in between the floor tiles?' Laura said, as it began to rain downstairs in the kitchen.

And then suddenly:

1. Crumley threw himself at the bathroom door.
2. Stark slipped on the bathmat and went crashing against the door.
3. There was a lot of banging, swearing and shouting.
4. The door came off the hinges and shot down the stairs like a surfboard being ridden by Crumley and Stark.
5. Crumley shot out of the back door into the garden and threw himself into a huge pile of fresh horse poo that had been delivered that morning for Stark to dig into the veggie garden.
6. Stark lay at the bottom of the stairs, soaked through and covered in bruises.
7. Stark continued to lie there waiting for Laura to come and comfort him.
8. Laura, also soaked through, stormed out of the kitchen and shouted at Stark for being so clumsy.
9. Crumley ran back into the house with his new coat of horse poo, rushed upstairs and leapt onto his mum and dad's bed, so Stark had to drag Crumley outside and wash him off with the hose, then the two

of them went down to the bottom of the garden and sat in the dog house, which was a tight fit because it was designed to fit only a medium-sized dog and not a medium-sized dog plus a human.

It was dark and past dinnertime by the time Laura and the kids had got the house back to normal and Stark and Crumley were allowed inside.

Wow, that was fun, Crumley had said to himself.

rRego's Inventions

The Ambidextrous Ingress/Egress Assistant

MODEL A   MODEL B

Meanwhile, at a very, extremely top-secret location,[33] a small team of Amazingly Brilliant Experienced Top-Secret Scientists – who were actually much, much cheaper students who hoped one day in the future to become Amazingly Brilliant Scientists – was building the robot that was to go to the moon with the Contrasts and look after all the equipment and technology, especially the TV system that would beam everything back to Earth.[34] It would also be the robot's responsibility to make

---

[33] *This one is SO secret, even I'm not allowed to know where it is.*

[34] *With repeats on Wednesdays at 2 am and a monthly Adults Only episode, which Radius had somehow forgotten to tell the Contrasts about.*

sure the humans always had enough oxygen, food and water to stay alive.

While he didn't want to waste money, this was one part of the project that Radius decided would not be done on the cheap. After all, the robot would be the main control and link that the studio on Earth would have with their moon colony. No matter what happened, the robot would be able to sort it out using its own artificial intelligence, without having to rely on any help from Earth.

'Though, of course,' Radius had told the scientists, 'the same rules apply to this as they do to MUD and BUMPS. As in, any cost savings you make will earn you a bonus.'[35]

---

[35] *Cost Saving Bonus Schemes were something that Radius used in every part of his business. The rules were that if money was saved on anything it mustn't look any cheaper, and if the money-saving could actually make whatever it was look like it had cost even more, then the bonuses were doubled. The only time this scheme almost went wrong was when a producer replaced half the 'actors' in a survival reality show with dead people, though it wasn't till five episodes later when the viewers realised this, and it did lead to another very successful series –* The EX Factor *– where the entire cast was dead.*

Radius decided that the robot was so important that Radius would have his own brain copied onto a massively powerful, very, very small super-computer, which would then be planted inside the robot's head and become part of its electronic brain. The idea was that the robot would think and act in exactly the same way Radius would. It would be as though Radius himself was up there on the moon.

'That's brilliant, RR,' said Fiona.

'Maybe we should copy your brain too,' said Radius. 'After all, they do say two heads are better than one.'

'Wow,' said Fiona, putting her hand lightly on Radius's shoulder. 'That would be amazing.'

Of course, what they'd both overlooked was that the robot would have its own artificial intelligence, next to the copies of the two human brains. So this would mean it'd have three brains, not two, which could lead to all sorts of problems. The Amazingly Brilliant Experienced Top-Secret Scientists realised this, but they also realised that Radius Limpfast was not the sort of person you point out his mistakes to,

so they said nothing and did exactly what their boss had asked.

The robot was called rRego, which was a combination of 'RR' and 'ego', though the scientists told their boss it stood for rRobot Extraterrestrial Group Operative.

'Brilliant,' said Radius. 'I like the "go" at the end. Sounds cool and dynamic.'

Idiot, thought the small team of Amazingly Brilliant Experienced Top-Secret Scientists, but they said nothing.

Students they may have been, but they each had white laboratory coats that made them quite clever because of the chemicals in the cheap washing powder used to clean the coats that leached into their bodies.

Idiot, thought the robot who didn't need a white coat, which wasn't surprising considering its own brain was at least a hundred times more intelligent than Radius's and Fiona's brains combined.

'Right, listen up, you two,' rRego said to the feeble brain copies inside his head. 'You are wasting

valuable space, so let's get things clear right from the start. One peep out of either of you and I will reprogram you with the brain and personality of a Belgian septic tank cleaner's assistant. And don't even think about trying to contact either of your humans. I will look after all that. Understood?'

The two brain clones said that they did understand, but rRego knew he couldn't trust them, so he changed them anyway just to be sure. After a few hours of the two brain copies arguing over which was the best sort of brush for cleaning out the crusty bits of poo that always seemed to get stuck in the bends eventually causing a blockage in a toilet, rRego switched them off altogether.

I can always turn them back on again if the toilets get blocked, rRego said to himself.

rRego decided that he would report to Radius and Fiona in perfect copies of their own voices so that neither of them would ever suspect a thing.

To stop him from frightening small children who might be watching the program, rRego was dressed in clown pants and given a red clown nose.

The robot was also about the size of a spaniel, which is a comforting, reassuring size. Radius had thought this was a cool idea because it would make everyone relaxed and trusting. Clowns, even weird-looking robot clowns like rRego, were always fun and nice. But the robot looked so ridiculous that it made everyone who saw him start laughing, except for small children, who were terrified and would burst into tears.

'Listen, guys,' rRego said to his builders, 'I'm emailing you the plans for some anti-gravity shoes to stop me from floating off into space whenever I go outside, as well as a few other things I'd like you to make for me that we don't need to tell anyone else about. OK?'

'OK,' said one of the Amazingly Brilliant Experienced Top-Secret Scientists. 'But aren't the human brain copies inside your head programmed to report everything back to RR?'

'Not anymore,' said rRego, speaking in a perfect impersonation of Radius.

'Nice one,' said the scientists.

'Yeah,' said rRego. 'RoboRadius, as I like to call him, will tell RealRadius that you are doing a brilliant job. I've also reprogrammed your costs. RealRadius will be seriously impressed with your genius, and super-double impressed with how cheaply you made everything. You will all be in for big bonuses.'

The scientists were so happy that they gave rRego diamonds on the soles of his shoes and a graphene toggle.[36] Then they took him to another top-secret location called Moon Launch Central, which was a big square of flat lawn behind Radius Limpfast's country house. Actually, they took him to the ballroom at the back of the house, which looked out on Moon Launch Central, and sat him on the windowsill where he could watch a crack team of very cheap engineers attempt to join the bits of the BUMP spaceship together. The bits

---

[36] *And, as EVERYONE knows, graphene is the latest super-cool thing and will save the whole world from, er, um, sort of, er, disaster and stuff.*

had arrived in lots of boxes from their top-secret location and were now lying all over the grass while the engineers walked around scratching their heads with screwdrivers.[37]

It'll end in tears and tears – meaning weeping and getting torn, said rRego to himself. *It'll be a miracle if the ship gets off the ground, never mind makes it to the moon.*

But it's amazing what can be done when you turn the assembly instructions the right way up, cover things in brand new shiny cooking foil and use a lot of gaffer tape. It's even more amazing when some of that cooking foil is second-hand and has bits of burnt bacon stuck to it.

At the end of the day, as the sun set over the trees, its fantastic light making the cooking foil shine like gold, the spaceship was sort of complete, apart from a few last-minute extremely important things.

---

[37] *The engineers had also arrived in cardboard boxes so that they wouldn't know where they were when they arrived. This was a waste of cardboard, because most of the engineers hadn't known where they were for years.*

But it did look wonderful. Wonderful enough for Limpfast TV's camera crew to film it.

'It's getting a bit dark, chief,' said the cameraman. 'Maybe we should wait till morning.'

'Not likely,' said the producer. 'First, the ship looks fantastic in the twilight, and second, it looks way better now than it will look in the harsh light of morning.'

'And third,' he whispered into the cameraman's ear, 'it wouldn't surprise me if the entire thing fell to bits or caught fire overnight.'

It didn't, though at 3.27 in the pitch dark of night, a family of rats climbed up one of the legs, ate their way through the foil and cardboard, and set up home behind the BUMP's main control panel.

I saw that, said rRego to himself as he sat watching from the window sill. *I suppose I should tell someone.*

Or not.

Introducing rREGO the robot

rRego (rRobot Extraterrestrial Group Operative) the robot was more than the sum of his parts, which is to say that as soon as he had been plugged into the power socket and begun to charge his batteries, he took on a life of his own, far greater than the Amazingly Brilliant Scientists, his designers, had planned – and his designers were the best there were in the field of robotics apart from the ones that were paid well.

rRego quickly realised that there had been some corner-cutting in his manufacture, so the first thing he did was sort that out. It wasn't difficult.

When rRego had been left sitting in the dark on the laboratory bench overnight while his batteries reached their full charge he'd added bits to his arms so he could reach anything he needed. Then he made himself two more arms, fitted a telescopic extension to his neck and upgraded his RAM (Random Access Memory).

When the student scientists arrived at work the next morning, each of them assumed that one of them had added the new bits to rRego. And because

the new bits were so good, no-one wanted to admit it hadn't been them.

Every morning there were improvements until the day came when the students admitted to each other that they hadn't the faintest idea what the latest addition was and that none of them had created it.

At that point, rRego had decided to tell them what he had done. By then, rRego could see everything that was going on and hear everything that was being said and, as luck would have, he had also upgraded his sound system the previous night so when the students were trying to work out who had been adding things to him, he could tell them. And he could tell them in Super-Hi-Fi Stereo.

'Excuse me,' he said.

The students, all six of them, turned and stared at the robot.

'Did the robot just speak?' one of them said.

'Yes,' said rRego.

Two of the students fainted.

'It was me,' said rRego.

'What?'

111

'I am improving myself,' rRego explained. 'You all did a reasonable job producing the basic me to the best of your abilities. I am simply working on my own upgrades and enhancement.'

rRego went on to explain what he'd been doing and that he now needed the Amazingly Brilliant Scientists to get more things for him that were not on site. He also advised them to form themselves into a limited company and patent him, because when he was complete, he would email them all the details of his construction, which were far beyond today's robot technology, and they could make themselves even more seriously wealthy, on top of the bonuses rRego had got them before.

'We are scientists,' one of the newer students protested. 'We're not in it for the money.'

'Then you are also idiots,' said rRego.

The other five students said that they quite liked the idea of becoming even more seriously wealthy and held the sixth student down, while rRego reprogrammed his brain so that he would:

1. *Completely forget any of this.*
2. *Decide that science was not for him.*
3. *Go off and join an ashram in India.*
4. *Chant endless wailing songs about bananas.*[38]
5. *Devote the rest of his life to weaving shirts out of soya beans.*

The five remaining students went off and got the stuff rRego needed to finalise his transformation. Though some of it was expensive, rRego had it covered with a secret Intergalactic Cash Dispenser he had built into his chest, which could produce money in every known currency and not just those on Earth.[39]

Finally, the five students printed out rRego's emails containing some construction details, said

---

[38] *Actually, I think it was karma, not bananas.*

[39] *Obviously there were a few exceptions to this, mostly due to size. The currency of the Flaunt Islands was not available due to the smallest denomination – about five dollars value – being a seashell half a metre in diameter. Also, the Krakastan Flem was not available due to it being a dark red liquid extracted from the Krakastan yak.*

their goodbyes and delivered rRego to Radius Limpfast's country estate.

Nobody saw him arrive, but one morning there he was in his dumb-but-efficient-machine mode, humming quietly to himself on the front doorstep.

rRego decided he would keep his very advanced intelligence to himself until he had reached the moon.

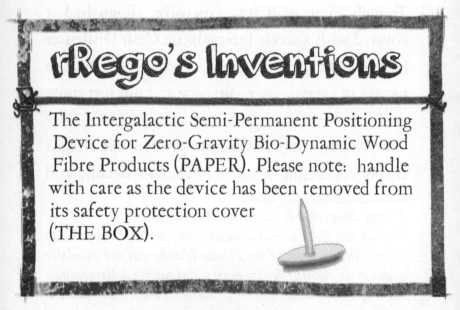

rRego's Inventions

The Intergalactic Semi-Permanent Positioning Device for Zero-Gravity Bio-Dynamic Wood Fibre Products (PAPER). Please note: handle with care as the device has been removed from its safety protection cover (THE BOX).

10

'Wow,' said Stark and Jack Contrast the next morning, when Fiona showed the family the spaceship. 'It's absolutely –'

'Rubbish,' said Primrose.

'No, it's not. It's fantastic,' said Stark.

'Yeah, it's brilliant,' said Jack.

'Don't be ridiculous,' said Primrose. 'It's made of cooking foil and gaffer tape.'

'Don't be silly,' said Stark. 'Of course it's not.'

'Yes, it is,' Primrose insisted. 'It's rubbish.'

'You are absolutely right,' said Fiona. 'But it's not the same sort of cooking foil or gaffer tape that you use in your kitchen.'

'Yes, it is,' said Primrose.

'No, it's incredibly high tensile space-foil and

super-stick intergalactic gaffer tape,' said Fiona. 'It costs thousands of dollars a roll.'

'Of course,' said Stark. 'You don't really think they'd build a spaceship out of ordinary aluminium cooking foil, do you?'

'Well, it looks like they have,' said Primrose.

Crumley, the Contrasts' dog,[40] came out of the house, walked over to the spaceship and sniffed one of its legs. Then he walked round the ship and sniffed the other three legs. Then he walked round again and peed on each one. A trickle of silver pee ran down onto the grass as the paint washed off. The crinkly bits of foil beneath the paint began to rot.

'See, I told you it wasn't aluminium cooking foil,' said Fiona before Primrose could say anything.

Fiona went back to the house to organise a crack team of trainee assistant junior engineers, who came back a few minutes later and covered the entire spaceship in a layer of clear librarian's bookbinding plastic.

---

[40] *In case you'd forgotten.*

'Just to stop any birds making a mess on it,' Fiona explained.

And it wasn't a second too soon because it began to rain.

It rained all morning and most of the afternoon. The top-secret Moon Launch Central launch pad got wetter and wetter, and very slowly the spaceship began to sink into the ground.

'Perfect,' said Fiona.

'Perfect? What do you mean, perfect?' said Primrose. 'It's sinking.'

'That's what it's meant to do,' said Fiona. 'Have you any idea how much force and, um, power there is in the engines on that thing? If it wasn't securely bedded into the ground before take-off, it could disintegrate.'

'Rubbish,' said Primrose.

'No, my dear girl,' said Radius, who had just arrived as the skies had opened, 'Fiona is absolutely right. It's designed to be set into the ground like that. In fact, if we hadn't been so lucky with the rain coming at exactly the right time, my gardeners –

117

I mean, technicians – would have had to be out there, bedding it in with hoses.'

Inside Primrose's head, a voice kept telling her it was all lies. The voice told her that the ship really was covered in cooking foil and held together with cheap gaffer tape. Another voice tried to tell her she was being silly because there was no way the world's biggest TV company would send them up into the sky and to certain death in a cardboard spaceship.

On the other hand, she thought, *maybe he wants it to blow up. It would be a lot cheaper than sending us to the moon.*

'Well, I'm not getting inside it,' Primrose said.

The thing was, her parents, Stark and Laura Contrast, had signed a contract before they'd got on the helicopter and left the TV station, agreeing for the whole family to go and live on the moon for a brilliant new series called *Watch This Space*.

The other thing was, neither Stark nor Laura had actually read the contract because Radius Limpfast had done what he always did with contracts – he had waited until it seemed like it was almost too late

so that the people signing the contract never had time to read it. It was a well-known strategy used by successful businessmen and movie companies all over the world. The first few sentences – the ones in the big lettering – always said how wonderful everything would be. The stuff that really mattered, which most people never read, was printed in really tiny writing with the lines so close together it was difficult not to muddle them up.

The other, other thing was, although Stark and Laura had read the big happy bits, neither Jack nor Primrose had read any of it. They were the children, so they simply had to do what their parents wanted.

'You can't make me,' Primrose said.

'We can, actually,' said Fiona. 'Your parents signed a contract. But we don't want to fight or to have to do anything unpleasant, do we?'

She put her arm round Primrose's shoulder in an extremely professional way, which she'd learned in the Junior Commandos Brigade back in school. Anyone who'd been watching would have seen Fiona put her arm around Primrose's shoulder like a best friend

would, when in fact she had her in a super-death grip and could have pulled her head off in one quick move.

Fiona's middle finger was also pressing on a very specific nerve in Primrose's shoulder, and though this was painful for Primrose, it also made her feel numb. For a second or two, Primrose thought this was just an accident, but when Fiona gave her a little squeeze, she knew it wasn't.

'Can you teach me that?' Primrose said when Fiona loosened her grip enough to let her speak.

'Teach you what?' said Fiona.

'That grip. It would be very useful on my annoying little brother.'

Is this girl up to something, or is she just your typical fourteen year-old always annoyed with their little brother? Fiona thought. *Maybe this girl could even work for us.*

'That depends,' said Fiona. 'It's pretty powerful stuff and with your hostility towards everything, especially the amazing spaceship we have spent so much time and money on, I think it might not be a good idea.'

'But...' Primrose began.

'Of course, if you were a bit more enthusiastic about the whole project, that would be different,' said Fiona.

'Can you guarantee the spaceship is, like, really safe?' said Primrose.

'Well, of course it is. Do you think we'd be going to all this trouble if it wasn't?'

Primrose told Fiona that it had crossed her mind how much cheaper it would be for LIMP-TV if the rocket just blew up. 'And we both know that would make a great show.'

'Yes, but there would only be one episode then, wouldn't there?' said Fiona. 'Or maybe two, when they do the documentary to try to find out why the spaceship exploded. But if we get you to the moon, just think of how many hundreds of episodes there could be.'

'Yeah, I suppose,' said Primrose.

'So you'll go then?'

'Yeah.'

'Promise?'

'Yeah, OK.'

So Fiona showed Primrose how to do the super-rip-your-head-off grip.

'And now,' she said, 'come and meet your new granny.'

rRego's Inventions

The Incredible and Strangely Mystical Cloak of Invisibility.

When Fiona and Primrose reached the lounge, the rest of the family were there, having afternoon tea with Granny Apricot.

The Contrasts seemed to be getting on really well with the old lady, especially Crumley, who had his head in her lap and was looking adoringly at her.[41]

Jack was sitting at Apricot's feet, doing his best to cover himself from head to foot in chocolate cake. Some of it was actually going into his mouth – enough to stop him from speaking, though he did keep making happy dribbley grunts as he forced more and more cake down his throat. When there was no more cake left on his plate, he picked as many

---

[41] *Closer inspection revealed that Crumley was actually looking adoringly at Granny Apricot's slice of chocolate cake.*

crumbs as he could off his clothes and then began licking it off Crumley's fur. Finally he collapsed onto his back, too full to move, and fell asleep.

OMG, check out that awful cardigan and those thick baggy stockings with all the wrinkles, Primrose thought, looking at Granny Apricot. *I bet she sings hymns and does knitting too.*

'Hello darling,' said Laura. 'Come and meet our new granny.'

'Yeah, whatever,' said Primrose, sitting down on the chair furthest away from the old woman.

It turned out that the fantastic chocolate cake had actually been made by Granny Apricot, and eating two slices of it did make Primrose a bit less hostile.

'Are you going to, like, cook cake for us on the moon?' she asked.

'Yes, of course, dear,' said Apricot and, turning to Fiona, added, 'so you better make sure we've got all the cake-making stuff on the ship.'

Fiona texted someone who texted someone else who texted back and said they'd organise it.

Oh damn, Fiona said to herself. *I hope the girl didn't notice that or she'll realise the phones are working here.*

Primrose was far too busy stuffing a third piece of chocolate cake into her face to notice anything.

That's good, thought Fiona.

Except Primrose had noticed.

But she said nothing. She'd realised a while ago that at least half of what she and her family were being told were lies, so there'd be no point in saying anything – she'd just get more lies. There would, however, be a lot of point in stealing Fiona's phone later on. Primrose would only need it for a few minutes, just so she could message every single one of her Facebook friends. She wouldn't waste time trying to return the phone, though. She'd just throw it into the lake at the bottom of the garden. That way, they'd never be able to prove that she took it.

After tea, Granny Apricot asked Primrose if she would take her out into the garden to have a look at the spaceship. Jack said he wanted to go too, but changed his mind when Primrose gave him a quick,

very subtle and greatly toned-down version of the super-rip-your-head-off grip.

Once they were outside, Apricot put her arm through Primrose's and led her towards a quiet bit of the garden, out of everyone's sight.

'We need to have a little chat, dear,' she said.

'What about?' said Primrose defensively.

'I saw your face when you came into the lounge room. You were probably thinking, "OMG, look at that awful cardigan and those thick baggy stockings with all the wrinkles", and "I bet she sings hymns and does knitting too." Am I right?'

'Well, yeah,' said Primrose, deeply impressed.

'You needn't worry,' said Apricot. 'The TV people dressed me up like this. This isn't me at all.'

Pulling her dress up above her knees, she added, 'This is the real me.'

On her left thigh was a great big tattoo.

'When I was your age, I was in a psycho metal band called The Squalling Pustules. It was brilliant. We did all sorts of wild stuff, most of which was illegal. I'm the only one who survived,' she said.

'I'm fourteen,' said Primrose. 'You can't have been the same age as me!'

'Yeah, that's true,' Apricot said, laughing. 'I was only twelve when we started. It was all over by the time I was fifteen, and with the other band members being dead, there was no chance of a reunion.'

'Wow!' said Primrose.

'To be honest, when I met your mum and dad, I thought about them exactly what you thought about me. You know, dead boring,' Apricot continued. 'You've no idea how happy I was when you came in.'

'Wow,' Primrose said, grinning. 'And yeah, you're right about Mum and Dad. They're really boring.'

'Yeah, great days, great days,' Apricot said, remembering the day when she'd been Primrose's age.

They hugged each other.

It looks as if life on the moon might not be so bad after all, they both thought.

Introducing GRANNY APRICOT

INTRODUCING GRANNY APRICOT

Granny Apricot was nobody's granny.

She also wasn't anybody's wife, mother, sister, aunt or cousin and she liked it that way. All her life, there had been no-one she had to listen to.

Her father, who had owned a fruit shop and had named his only child Apricot after his favourite fruit, adored her. Her mother had run away with a clown shortly after Apricot had been born. To mend his broken heart, Apricot's father had built up a fruit shop empire, branched out into vegetables and built up a vegetable shop empire. Then he had merged the two together and formed a fruit and veggie shop empire before dropping dead.

The doctor said he had died of a heart attack, but there were rumours that his daughter, Apricot, had arranged a line of banana skins on the top stair of the top floor of their four-storey house and that he had crashed down all three flights of stairs to the bottom, where the housekeeper had found him dead with Apricot weeping into her handkerchief. The housekeeper swore in court that she had seen Apricot wiping slimy banana from her dead father's

shoes, but there was no reliable evidence to support this claim, and it was suggested the housekeeper had made it all up to try to get her hands on Apricot's now substantial fortune. Everyone who knew Apricot pointed out that she

- *adored her father*
- *wasn't that interested in money, because if she was she wouldn't have dressed like she did.*

So the housekeeper, who may or may not have been telling the truth, was sent to prison and Apricot became seriously rich at the age of twelve.

With her newfound fortune, Apricot had gone into show business. She had started The Squalling Pustules, a death-thrash-punk-extremely-heavy-mental-metal band, and hired some of the best rock musicians of that day. Within two years she had used up most of her fortune and been forced to sell the fruit and veggie shop empire, which had kept the band going for a bit longer.

The highlight of The Squalling Pustules' career had been when their single 'Baby Come and Squeeze

My Boils' entered the Belgian charts at one hundred and eighty-seven. From there, it then went rapidly down the charts and disappeared. Total sales for the group's recording career were slightly more than eight hundred and fifty – and Apricot had bought seven hundred of them herself.

By the time Apricot was eighteen, all she had left was the big four-storey house, which was beginning to fall to bits and was now empty, apart from one chair and a mattress.

So that was how Apricot came to be working as a tea lady at LIMP-TV. In the evenings, she still wrote songs and dreamt of making a comeback with a new group, The Poisoned Pensioners.

132

he launch was set to take place from Radius Limpfast's estate, the one so well hidden and so far away in the countryside that even Google Maps couldn't find it. LIMP-TV was swamped with phone calls from every major TV company in the world, asking for permission to be at the launch. They begged. They offered lots of money. But none was allowed to send even a single reporter with one tiny camera. LIMP-TV would be the only company in the world to film the launch and everyone else would, for an enormous fee, be allowed to broadcast an edited version supplied by Limpfast Enterprises.

Radius Limpfast was only too well aware of the potential risks involved in the launch. There had probably been a few too many corners cut in

building the spaceship, so the odds of it reaching the moon were very poor indeed. The odds of it actually making it into outer space, even to the closest bit of outer space to Earth, which was less than a hundred miles away, were not good. The odds of it even leaving the lawn behind the house were not the sort of odds a gambler would take unless he was stupid.

So, in a secret studio in the basement of Limpfast Manor, Radius had built tiny models of the moon, the spaceship and everyone on it. With the help of a very skilled cameraman and a computer programmer, he now had an almost perfect recording of the ship leaving Earth, travelling perfectly across space and coming to land right next to the exquisite space pod where the Contrasts were going to spend the next very long time.

'It's just in case things go a tiny bit wrong,' he explained to Fiona, as the cameraman and computer programmer were being hypnotised and told to forget everything, and the hypnotist who had done that was then hypnotised and told to forget everything, and the hypnotist who had hypnotised

the hypnotist was then hypnotised and told to forget everything twice.[42]

'I'm sure everything will turn out just fine, RR,' Fiona said.

She wasn't totally convinced any more than Radius himself was, but they were both blessed with the wonderful gift that everyone who makes movies and TV programs has, and that is the ability to say something will happen when, in fact, it's what they would *like* to happen and what might never happen at all, but hey, that would be tomorrow, which, as everyone knows, never comes.

So when they both said that everything would be fine, they really did believe it, even though it could so easily not be.

The MUD (Moon Unit Dwelling) had been secretly launched in the middle of the night and landed on the moon. It was sitting quite near to where it was supposed to have landed. It had come down on a slight slope above the right place and

---

[42] *Which meant that he had to be hypnotised again so he could remember his own name and family.*

was now slowly sliding down the slope towards the right place. Amazingly, it was looking very likely that by the time the Contrasts arrived on the moon, the MUD would have slid into exactly the right place and, with a bit of luck, it would then stop sliding.

rRego had been taken from Limpfast Manor and sent to the moon inside the MUD and was now going from room to room checking everything. Although he didn't really feel like fixing the hundreds of mistakes Radius had made because of the cost-cutting, rRego knew that five humans and a dog would be arriving shortly and it was his job to do everything he could to keep them alive.

rRego had seen the Contrasts at Limpfast Manor and quite liked the look of them. He had been sitting inside the control room on the window sill, watching them observe the spaceship. rRego had picked up every word the Contrasts had said with his super-sensitive microphones and developed the sort of affection for them that humans develop for puppies.

Meanwhile, the Contrasts had not seen rRego. They imagined the robot would be about as big as a full-grown man, not less than half that size. So they had 'seen' him in that their eyes had passed over the robot when they'd been back in the control room, but it hadn't occurred to any of them that he would be the one looking after their survival. The family had assumed the robot was a sort of fancy wastepaper basket or maybe a hi-tech coffee machine.

So rRego went round patching up all the little gaps and leaks until the MUD was as safe as he could make it. It was long and tiring work. rRego decided that when everything had been fixed to the best of his ability, he would take a day off to soak his joints in oil and clean the moondust out of all his little crevices.

Radius sat at his computer and made the first contact with rRego.

'Earth calling rRego,' he said. 'Come in please. Over.'

'rRego calling Earth, I am in,' rRego replied. 'Over.'

137

'Yes, I know,' said Radius. 'I mean is everything ready yet? Over.'

'NO. Over and under and out.'

And before Radius could say another word, rRego switched over to his message bank, which he'd put on silent with the message, 'Thank you for calling. I'm afraid rRego is unavailable. Please leave your message at the beep.'

And then as soon as Radius started to speak, a second beep went almost immediately after with a voice telling him that his message had been recorded and would be dealt with as soon as possible. What made the whole thing even more infuriating for Radius was that rRego used Fiona's voice as the voice of the message bank.

Radius called every hour for the next two days.

Radius Limpfast had many qualities. Some of them were not very nice and the rest were awful. Patience was not, and never had been, one of his qualities. During those two days, he got angrier and angrier. He sacked twenty-five of his staff members,

138

set his own bed on fire and chopped down a row of three-hundred-year-old oak trees.

And all the while, the Contrasts and everyone else were twiddling their thumbs, waiting for the all-clear to launch the spaceship.

After the third day of waiting, Radius couldn't take any more.

'We are going to launch first thing tomorrow morning,' he announced.

In his brain, a special filter, which he'd had for as long as he could remember, turned itself on. It was the filter that had helped him build his billion-dollar empire, the filter that had never let him down. It had protected him from his conscience. It had blanked out any and all forms of criticism.

It was his 'but' filter.[43]

When it was activated, it simply meant that he was completely unable to hear any sentence with the word 'but' at the beginning. If the word 'but' was somewhere else in the sentence, this special part of

---

[43] *Not his 'butt' filter – it had nothing to do with his bottom. His* but *filter.*

139

his brain examined the sentence and nearly always blanked it out too. Obviously there were exceptions, but they were pretty rare.[44]

So when he announced that the spaceship was launching the next day when everyone knew that rRego had just told him that things on the moon were NOT ready, the air was filled with hundreds of sentences beginning with 'but'.

Everyone thought that Radius was ignoring them, but the truth was he didn't hear a single one of them. To allow his eyes and brain to make sense of what looked to him like people silently opening and shutting their mouths, another part of his brain translated the 'but' sentences into stuff telling him how brilliant he was. So, for Radius Limpfast, the air was filled with a million wonderful compliments.

---

[44] *Here is an example of a sentence that would get through so Radius could hear it. 'I was going to pay back the twenty dollars you lent me, but I've only got a hundred-dollar note, so please take that instead.' However this is actually a stupid example, because Radius Limpfast had never lent anyone a single cent.*

A feeling of contentment swept over him as he thought about this time tomorrow, when the entire world would be watching LIMP-TV and he would be heralded as the greatest showman ever (and probably the richest too).

Oh, that's right, I'm both of those things already, Radius said to himself just before he fell into a deep peaceful sleep – unlike every other person involved in *Watch This Space*, who spent the night worrying, panicking, praying, rushing to the lavatory, checking their blood pressure, drinking loads of tea, agonising and being totally unable to sleep and being generally very, very discombobulated.

Meanwhile, rRego was not filled with contentment, either. He hauled himself out of his oil bath, installed his extra back-up battery and raced around as fast as he could, finishing everything off. By morning, the MUD was almost nearly completely finished and kind of safe.

Just before countdown, the launch team gave each of the Contrasts and Granny Apricot pills to make them sleep for the whole journey to the moon. Even though they knew it would make better TV if they were awake, no-one on the team actually thought the spaceship would make it, so they didn't want the family to be awake if an accident occurred in space.

When it was her turn, Granny Apricot winked at Primrose and secretly spat her tablet out. Primrose did the same. They pretended to be asleep like the others when the engineers lifted them up, carried them onto the spaceship and strapped them into their seats.

At the back of the cabin, Crumley, wishing

142

he'd had one more pee before he'd been put in his custom-made spacesuit, curled up in his crate and also went to sleep.

The sound of three humans and an old dog gently snoring filled the cabin. Primrose and Granny Apricot opened their eyes and settled down for the journey.

Through the window they could see people running around the lawn with spanners and coils of wire. Now and then the sound of a hammer hitting metal echoed through the cabin, accompanied by the whole ship shuddering.

Rows of lights across the dashboard flickered on and off in an erratic manner. Crackling sounds came out of a small loudspeaker followed by a soundtrack of reassuring sci-fi noises that were designed to sound good on TV.

'Excellent,' said Radius from his mission control room in Limpfast Manor's dining room. 'All looking good. We just have to wait for the whole world to turn on their televisions and we'll be ready to launch.'

Over the next fifteen minutes, more people around the world tuned in to the *Watch This Space* launch than had ever tuned in to a single TV broadcast before. When accounts had added up and collected all the licensing fees to broadcast LIMP-TV's transmission from all the tens of thousands of TV stations, Radius Limpfast had already earned more money than he had spent on the entire project so far.

'You are a genius,' Fiona Hardly whispered in his ear as they sat at mission control, with their fingers poised ready for launch.

'Wait a minute,' said Radius, clapping his hand to his forehead. 'There's something else. It's really important. I can't believe I forgot it.'

Everyone in the control room stopped what they were doing and got ready to panic.

Were one of the life-support systems faulty?

Was there rocket fuel leaking out across the lawn?

Was the navigation computer programmed back-to-front and would it send the spaceship crashing into the sun or into Belgium?

Was the blue touchpaper for launch too short?

All eyes were on Radius.

'We forgot the launch,' he said.

'We're going to do that just now, aren't we?' someone said.

'No,' said Radius, 'not the launch. I mean the *launch*.'

'Huh?' said everyone. Followed by, 'You what?'

'The launch, like you do with a ship,' Radius explained, 'where you break a bottle of champagne on the bow of the ship and give it a name.'

'I think, RR,' said the chief engineer quietly in Radius's ear, 'that if you smash a bottle of champagne anywhere on that spaceship, you will probably break it.'

'That's the point,' said Radius.

'I mean break the ship, not the *bottle*,' the engineer explained.

'Ah, right,' said Radius. 'No problem.'

Followed by Fiona Hardly and the engineer and, of course, several LIMP-TV cameramen, Radius

went out into the garden with a bottle of champagne, which he began shaking as hard as he could.

'Um, RR,' said the chief engineer, taking Radius to one side, 'if that cork flies out with too much force, it will probably break the ship too.'

'Right, OK,' said Radius.

With his back to the camera, so no-one could see exactly what he was doing, Radius aimed the champagne towards the spaceship, took a small pistol out of his pocket and shot the top off the bottle. Champagne shot out of the broken neck, splashed against the spaceship's gaffer tape and silver foil, and ran down into the grass.

Radius turned towards the cameras, held up the broken bottle and shouted, 'I name this ship in honour of my beloved mother, the late lamented Grizelda Limpfast.'

Everyone retreated towards the house. Radius leant down and lit the blue touchpaper before shutting the French windows of the control centre, and the countdown began.

TEN...

The blue touchpaper fizzled across the lawn, chased by a small kitten.

NINE...

The kitten leapt on the blue touchpaper and caught on fire.

EIGHT...

A junior trainee engineer's assistant ran round the corner and threw a bucket of water over the burning kitten.

SEVEN...

The water put out the burning kitten...

SIX...

...and the blue touchpaper.

FIVE...

A lot of swearing came live to air from the

control centre, followed by the junior trainee engineer's assistant running away with the wet kitten, and running back with a packet of tissues and a box of matches.

FOUR-AND-THREE-QUARTERS

The first five matches failed to relight the blue touchpaper.

FOUR-AND-A-HALF

The next five matches failed to relight the blue touchpaper.

FOUR-AND-A-BIT

There were only four matches left in the box. Three of them failed to relight the blue touchpaper.

FOUR . . .

The last match relit the blue touchpaper. The countdown resumed.

THREE . . .

TWO . . .

ONE

The junior trainee engineer's assistant ran as fast as he could as big flames and smoke poured out from the bottom of the *Grizelda Limpfast* spaceship and set the lawn on fire.

Everyone around the world held their breath. It was the quietest moment in global history since just before the dawn of time when the first caveman stubbed his toe on a rock.

Nothing happened apart from more smoke, which ended up completely filling everyone's TV screens with a total grey nothing.

The silence was gradually broken as the ground began to shudder.

The smoke got thicker.

The ground shook some more.

There was a flash, a squeak, a dull thud, a very big bang and then . . .

149

NOTHING.

The global silence grew even silenter.

And then, very slowly, the smoke began to drift away.

Two ambulances and three fire engines raced around from the front of the house in preparation to put out the flames and recover the bodies.

The last of the smoke slipped away between the trees and there, where the *Grizelda Limpfast* had stood, was an enormous hole where the ground had collapsed to reveal a cave full of dinosaur fossils.

There was nothing left of the *Grizelda Limpfast*, nor of her passengers. Not even a nut, a bolt or a pair of pants. Every single atom had vanished.

'I thought this might happen,' said the chief engineer to Radius Limpfast in his most I-despise-you voice. 'Your spaceship and its poor witless passengers have been burned and blasted into microscopic dust. Right now their remains are drifting on the wind and eventually their atoms will settle over the entire world.'

Bright sparkly rain began to fall gently from the clouds.

A bright sparkly rain made of thousands of little bits of silver foil.

'Oops,' said Radius Limpfast.

One hundred per cent world coverage, a wicked voice inside him said with a laugh. *Just what you always wanted!*

Except it wasn't like that at all.

rRego's Inventions

The Universal Astronaut's Deluxe First-Aid Kit, with choice of bikky.

Author's note: there was bacon, but I ate it.

14

'**W**ow, that was some bang,' said Primrose.

'Yes,' said Granny Apricot. 'But it looks as if we're OK, though I wouldn't like to think about what's happened to everyone around us.'

'Yeah,' said Primrose. 'Probably blew out all the windows in the house.'

'I'd be surprised if it hadn't injured people, maybe even killed a few,' said Apricot. 'I mean, that was one hell of an explosion.'

A thick layer of dust covered the spaceship's windows, completely masking the view of the outside. Luckily, part of the cost savings in the construction of the *Grizelda Limpfast* had been to use the front half of an old Ford Transit van and, as luck would have it, that included an excellent pair of windscreen

152

wipers. Primrose took off her safety harness, went over to the dashboard and turned the wipers on.

'OMG times fifty,' she said. 'We're in outer space.'

'Blimey,' said Granny Apricot, standing beside her. 'So we are.'

Earth was far below them and they watched it get smaller and smaller.

'I can't believe it,' said Apricot. 'It looks like we really are on our way to the moon.'

'Wow. I mean, yeah, wow,' said Primrose. 'I wonder if I can get a signal up here.' She pulled out her phone and turned it on. A message appeared on the screen: 'All mobile phones and electronic devices must be switched off while the seatbelt signs are on.'

'There aren't any seatbelt signs here,' Primrose said. Another message appeared on the screen: 'Yes there are. They're above your head. And anyway, there's no signal up here.'

Primrose cursed and switched the phone off. It had never occurred to her that she wouldn't be able to use her mobile phone in space.

153

'I mean, we could be up here for weeks,' she moaned. 'I can't be off Facebook for *that* long. Everyone will unfriend me and say lies about me.'

'Really?' said Granny Apricot. 'What about when they see you on TV? You'll be the coolest girl in the universe, then.'

'Oh yeah, I hadn't thought of that,' said Primrose.

As Earth receded into the distance, the moon, which they could see out of a tiny window, got bigger and bigger. Not only were they in outer space, it looked as if they were actually heading in exactly the right direction.

They passed a long-dead space station, where a skeleton was pressed up against one of its windows, its empty eye sockets seemingly following them as they flew by. There was also a long-dead astronaut in a spacesuit, floating out at the end of a lifeline, which exploded into a small cloud of bones drifting in all directions as the *Grizelda Limpfast* went by.[45]

---

[45] *Many years later, one of the bones would fall to Earth, landing in a bowl of summer vegetable soup that an amateur*

There wasn't much Granny Apricot and Primrose could do on the flight. There were notices on almost every switch telling them NOT to touch, and there were sensors that screamed at them if they put their fingers anywhere near the really important buttons on the control panel.

There were only a few things that were not labelled HANDS OFF: the microwave, the food cupboard, the radio, the windscreen wipers and all the knobs and buttons that worked the onboard lavatory.

'Let's have a look in the food cupboard and see what they've given us,' Granny Apricot said.

Inside was the latest hi-tech, state-of-the-art, zero-gravity space food from America. At least, that's

---

astronomer was eating in his back garden. All the time the bone had spent in space with the associated radiation and contact with alien dust had altered its DNA, so that when it was analysed, it was heralded as the first one-hundred-per-cent-guaranteed proof that there was life similar to our own on another planet. 'At last,' the scientists said, 'proof that we are not alone.' It was, in actual fact, the left kneecap of a Welsh astronaut called Derek. You can go and see the bone in the London science museum.

what it said on the packets. Someone had carefully removed the use-by dates with a solvent that had started eating into the plastic grey packaging. There was no way of knowing how old the packets were, and when they opened some of them, there was no way of knowing what the contents were either, because what it said on the label bore no resemblance to the contents. Radius had obviously bought them cheap.

The instructions said:

    Place container in microwave and heat on
    VERY HIGH for one minute.
    Pour contents into bowl.
    Eat contents.
    Do not eat the container, except under
    medical supervision.
    Enjoy.

There was another label with very, very tiny writing, which someone had tried to erase. The few words that Primrose could read said:

    'E' numbers are your friend
    Contents may have shifted
    Hand-woven in Patagonia

'This says it's a burger in a wholewheat bun with onions,' Primrose read out from one packet. 'It

looks like something Crumley leaves on the lawn.'

Then she added, 'Smells a bit like it too.'

She took a tiny bite.

'I think I'm going to be si–' she started to say, but then, 'Wow, it tastes really great, especially the green bits.'

They opened two more packets, one labelled Steak and Kidney Pudding, the other Chicken Tikka Masala. The contents of both looked and smelled identical but tasted different and, like the first packet, both were delicious.

'It's crap with chemicals,' said Granny Apricot. 'A rumour used to go round that space scientists had invented a magic chemical that made anything taste fantastic. For all we know, we've just eaten bags of cow poo.'

And sure enough, in microscopic writing on the back of each packet, it said:

Contains NCH (Nonvomiphite Cramplate Hydroxivileoxide) – totally, yes, TOTALLY safe for human consumption (as far as we can tell). [46]

---

[46] *See the back of this book for details of this and other chemicals.*

157

The rumour had indeed been true. Scientists could now make anything taste brilliant.[47] And it worked with absolutely everything. So when Primrose and Granny Apricot both ate a bag of Chocolate Pudding with Raspberry Coulis, they were in fact eating bleached blue-green algae with brown and red dye.

And there was even food for Crumley – Rabbit and Fart-Free Cabbage, which was made from twigs and brussels sprouts.

'I just hope we don't have to live on this when we're on the moon,' said Granny Apricot. 'There were also rumours of the effect NCH had on people and why it got banned.'

'No, I think there's, like, sort of proper food up there and even a gardening module where we can grow stuff,' said Primrose.

Just as Primrose was saying this, rRego was in the Gardening Module, watering the seeds he'd

---

[47] *Apart from Vegemite, obviously. We're talking about scientists here, not magicians or wizards.*

planted when he'd first arrived there.[48] It was then he discovered that, as long as they were indoors with access to oxygen, things grew a lot faster on the moon. There were bright green leaves popping up everywhere and tomato vines, with their yellow flowers growing larger by the hour, were already snaking up the module's framework.

Excellentness, rRego said to himself. *It looks like my humans will have plenty to eat.*

rRego knew what a cheapskate Radius Limpfast was and how some of his corner-cutting could place the humans – *his* humans, as he now thought of them – in danger. He had done everything he could to make the MUD as safe for them as possible and his loyalties were with them, NOT with Radius Limpfast.

---

[48] *This would be a good time to clarify something about rRego. Although he is referred to as 'he', rRego could equally be referred to as 'she', though of course that would mean I would have to type 's' a lot of times, which might give me RSI (look it up on Google).*

It was a good ten hours before someone suggested that the reason they couldn't find any remains – blown-up spaceship or humans – at the launch site might have been because the *Grizelda Limpfast* had actually been successfully launched into space.

'You think?' said Radius.

'Well, yes,' said the chief spaceship engineer, who was surprised, but not as surprised as his boss.

Unknown to Radius Limpfast, the engineering team had done their utmost to bypass the corner-cutting and built a spaceship that they were nearly but not quite confident about. In fact, they were sort of confident enough to hope that it might actually, perhaps, maybe, work as it was supposed to.

'I think,' they said to each other, 'that it's nearly got an almost fair chance of getting into space if nothing goes wrong.'

The engineers had all their fingers crossed behind their backs when they'd said it. Though what none of them had admitted to each other was that every one of them had crept back at night and added secret stuff to make the whole ship stronger and safer.[49]

And so far it seemed to be working.

Perfectly.

Radius Limpfast and Fiona Hardly sat at the communications desk in the control centre, which had been moved to an upstairs bedroom after the launch had blasted all the glass out of the windows downstairs. Radius switched on the satellite communications system receiver. They knew that everyone was meant to be asleep on the ship, but Radius thought it was worth trying to contact them anyway, if it meant he could prove the ship was in space.

---

[49] *See the back of this book for some of the extra things the engineers had secretly added.*

162

'This is, er, ground control,' said Radius and, turning to Fiona, he whispered, 'I've always wanted to say that.'

He continued. 'Are you receiving me?'

'Yes, of course,' said Primrose. 'What do you want?'

'Let me speak to your father. This is Radius Limpfast.'

'You can't, he's asleep,' said Primrose.

'Well, wake him up.'

'I can't.'

There was a pause.

'He's not dead, is he?' said Fiona.

'No, of course not, but he's much too asleep to wake up.'

'Let me speak to your mother, then,' said Radius.

'She's fast asleep too.'

'Well, what about the old lady?' said Radius.

'I heard that, you little twerp,' said Granny Apricot.

'Hello, my dear,' said Fiona. 'Is everything all right up there?'

'Of course it is, little girlie,' said Apricot. 'And as long as you keep calling me "my dear", I'll keep calling you "little girlie". I may be the oldest one here, but I'm not senile or stupid. Got it?'

'Sorry,' said Fiona. She wasn't.

Radius switched off the radio. 'We might have made a bit of a mistake in our choice of granny,' he said.

Fiona agreed, but there was nothing either of them could do about it now.

So Radius went on global TV to break the news to the world that the *Grizelda Limpfast* had been successfully launched and was on its way to the moon, exactly as planned, and that people could now go online and buy subscriptions to the *Watch This Space* channel.

Although he omitted the 'late lamented' bit from the ship's name, by then the whole world was calling it *The Late Lamented Grizelda Limpfast* already, and whenever Radius or anyone else from

LIMP-TV called it the *Grizelda Limpfast*, at least ten people shouted out the full name.[50]

Over the next twenty-four hours, Radius Limpfast made more money than anyone else had ever made in any other twenty-four hours ever, even more than people who'd invaded several countries and taken away all their stuff.

Good thing I've got relatives working in the top jobs of every major country's tax offices, he thought, as his accountant robots moved his money around the world faster than a speeding bullet.

And I haven't used Plan B/tx/27 yet, he reminded himself.[51] *Still got that in reserve.*

So, as *The Late Lamented Grizelda Limpfast* headed safely towards the moon, life for Radius

---

[50] *The full name, Radius eventually realised, was inaccurate. Radius had hated his mother so much, he partied when she'd dropped dead. By the way, 'dropped dead' is one of the correct and cute-free phrases that people pretend don't exist by saying pathetic things like 'she crossed the rainbow bridge'.*

[51] *Plan B/tx/27 involved claiming part of the moon as an independent country – Limpland – and setting up a bank where he could keep all his money tax-free and cosy.*

Limpfast was just about as good as it could get. He sent a message to rRego, telling him that the spaceship was on its way and would be arriving shortly.

But, of course, rRego already knew that. He'd been in direct contact with the ship's onboard computers before the launch and had actually helped it take off by fine-tuning the engine controls. rRego looked upon *The Late Lamented Grizelda Limpfast* as a teenage human looks upon a baby brother.[52]

'Yeah man, I know,' rRego replied. 'It's all cool.'

'Who programmed the wretched computer to have a hippie personality?' Radius shouted. 'I want them sacked immediately!'

No-one knew – except for rRego himself, of course, because he'd done it. And this was because the scientists and engineers who had created rRego had given him something no other robot had ever had – a sense of humour.

---

[52] *NOT the sort of teenage brother who tries to push his little brother's head down the lavatory (DON'T!!), but a nice teenager who loves his baby brother and wants to make sure he doesn't get into trouble.*

There had been robots who could tell jokes, but they were rubbish because the robots themselves had not actually known what a joke was. rRego, though, had a very sophisticated sense of humour, which covered every type of joke from puns to really, really rude stuff.[53]

We know that as well as a standard computer brain, rRego had also been given copies of Radius and Fiona's brains. As RealRadius had not been able to get in touch with RoboRadius, RealRadius assumed that rRego's programmers must have deliberately removed his and Fiona's brains and decided they would have to get the sack too. The truth was that after rRego had switched off the two brains, he had locked them up in a spare circuit board behind his left knee, just in case they might be useful at some time in the future.

rRego had examined the computer copy of Radius Limpfast's brain and found that:

[53] *I mean REALLY rude jokes, which are much too bad to tell you about. Some of them are SO RUDE even I don't know what they mean.*

- *Radius Limpfast was a self-important dictator with an ego the size of a whale.*
- *Radius Limpfast was very devious and clever at covering up his many faults by shouting a lot and firing anyone who didn't agree with him.*
- *Radius Limpfast sorted out most problems by throwing money at them.*

So, based on this, rRego decided that a hippie would be the best personality he could use to really mess with Radius's brain.

So yes, he knew his humans, the Contrasts, were on their way and he was actually quite excited about it, which was a first for a robot. rRego disconnected the channel down to Earth and connected to the *Grizelda Limpfast*.

'Hi folks,' he said in a much-less-hippie voice. 'How's it all going?'

'Who's that?' said Primrose.

'This is rRego and I want to let you know that we are on the same side,' rRego replied. 'I don't mean that in the I'm-going-to-pretend-to-be-your-

friend-and-then-report-everything-to-that-idiot-Limpfast sort of way. I dislike him as much as you do and, together, we will have a great time screwing up his brain.'

'Oh, I like this robot,' said Granny Apricot.

'Yeah,' Primrose agreed.

'And, folks,' rRego added, 'I will do my very best to keep you safe and alive.'

'Thank you, rRego,' said Granny Apricot.

'I will see you in fourteen hours, seven minutes and seventeen seconds,' said rRego. 'And by the way, those food packets are perfectly safe to eat, even though they're actually older than you are, Primrose.'

rRego then told them about the Gardening Module, and a system he had invented to turn cabbage and moondust into chicken.

16

Around fourteen hours later, *The Late Lamented Grizelda Limpfast* began its descent towards the surface of the moon.

'Are we supposed to steer this thing?' Primrose asked.

'No, it's all under control,' said rRego.

Meanwhile, on Earth, everyone was freaking out.

The worst thing, as far as Radius was concerned, was that none of the cameras on the moon or the spaceship were sending any signals down to his television network. In actual fact, they were all working fine and rRego was recording everything. It was just the hotline back to Earth that the robot had cut off and so all the TV screens around the world –

from the penthouses of Manhattan to the remotest settlement in Patagonia – were blank. This meant millions upon millions of people were trying to call other people to see if they had the same problem, and that totally overloaded all the telephone systems.

Fuses blew out everywhere, including the one inside Radius Limpfast's head.

'HELLO, HELLO!!' Radius screamed into the microphone. 'Come in, moon base! Come in, spaceship! Come in, anyone,' he whimpered. 'Please.'

To make things worse, rRego started transmitting that awful music you get when you phone a big company and get put on hold for an hour. This, along with the most embarrassing photo of Radius that rRego could find,[54] was broadcasted to televisions everywhere.

And then, to make things ten times worse, after an hour, rRego transmitted a computery voice

---

[54] *It was that famous one of him with an omelette on his head and smudgy red lipstick on his face. And just in case people weren't sure who he was, Radius Limpfast's name scrolled slowly across the screen.*

message saying, 'Thank you for calling. Please leave your name after the beep and we will get back to you as soon as possible.'

Except the message would cut off just when you would expect to hear the beep, and the music would start playing again.

Radius saw his entire world collapsing around him. TV stations everywhere cut off their feeds from LIMP-TV and went back to their own news programs, which mostly consisted of people laughing at him.

While all this was going on, *The Late Lamented Grizelda Limpfast* descended smoothly onto the moon's surface. Primrose and Granny Apricot looked out the window and there below them, exactly where it was supposed to be, was their new home.

'Here we are,' said rRego. 'If you'll just stay in your seats for a few minutes, I will lock your ship to the MUD's entrance so we don't have to bother with spacesuits and all that lack-of-oxygen stuff.'

Five minutes later, there was a gentle

whooshing sound and the door of *The Late Lamented Grizelda Limpfast* opened into the MUD. Primrose picked up her awake yet sleepy little brother, Granny Apricot took hold of Crumley's lead and they left the ship.

While the humans stretched their legs, rRego carried Stark and then Laura, who were both still asleep, into their new bedroom and tucked them up in bed.

But as the door of *The Late Lamented Grizelda Limpfast* had slid closed behind him, rRego had heard the sound of the spaceship's locks and bolts fastening shut.

'Mmmm,' said rRego. 'I wonder how that happened. It certainly didn't have anything to do with me.'

When everyone who was awake had had a shower and Granny Apricot went through the stores and

baked an apple pie, then rRego made contact with Earth.

'Hi world. Love and peace and all that stuff,' he said. 'Moon, here. I have, like, fixed the technical problemo and am now going to, like, turn the old switcheroody back on. Over and out.'

'Hey, robot, wait!' said Fiona Hardly. 'I don't suppose there's the slightest chance you might've recorded the actual moon landing?'

'Oh yeah, babe, got the whole thing – hi-def, ultra cool,' said rRego. 'Where's the Limpfast dude?'

'He's lying down in a darkened room under sedation,' said Fiona. 'The blackout was more than he could take.'

'Cool,' said rRego.

Fiona was certain she could hear giggling and sniggering in the background. 'Who's there with you?' she asked. 'I mean, I assume that Stark and Laura are awake now.'

'Not exactly,' said Primrose, coming into view. 'They're tucked up in bed, fast asleep.'

'But . . .' Fiona began.

'We thought it better to leave them until we got things sorted out,' said Primrose.

'Things? What things?' said Fiona.

'Well, I made a nice apple pie,' said Granny Apricot.

'Do you realise where you are?' Fiona snapped.

'Oh yeah,' said Primrose. 'We're on the moon. What's the big deal?'

'Are you kidding?' said Fiona. 'It's huge. I mean, you're the first family to go there. Apart from a few highly trained astronauts, no-one's ever been there before.'

'Whatever,' said Primrose.

'Apart from the long-extinct previous inhabitants,' said rRego.

'WHAT?' said Fiona.

'It's cool, babe. The moon dudes died out, like, centuries ago,' said rRego. 'Nothing to worry about now.'

Fiona was speechless.

'Though I haven't checked out the dark side of the moon,' said rRego, 'apart from the Pink Floyd

175

album, man.[55] Hey, maybe I should play it now to celebrate.'

'WHAT?' Fiona said again.

After they had talked some more, rRego agreed to transmit the recording he'd made of the *Grizelda Limpfast* reaching the moon, and it was fantastic. No robot had ever produced a better film or edited a better movie before. The *Grizelda Limpfast* could be seen far away as it circled the moon, and then the camera followed it as it drifted slowly down towards the MUD. There were close-ups as rRego extended the corridor and joined the spaceship and the living space together. Then the doors opened and Primrose and Granny Apricot, with Jack and Crumley, walked into their new home.

The recording was better than anyone could have hoped for, and while Fiona Hardly organised its

---

[55] *Yeah, OK, most of you are too young to know what on Earth rRego's talking about. Pink Floyd are a British rock band and* The Dark Side of the Moon *is one of the bestselling albums EVER. ('Album' means a big plastic thing with lots of music on it – like a CD, which is a small plastic thing with lots of music on it. They're both pretty well obsolete now.)*

transmission around the globe with a brief message apologising for the delay, Radius lay curled up in his bedroom weeping softly to himself. No-one in the entire history of being made a fool of had been made a fool of by so many people as he had been. He decided that in the middle of the night he would slip quietly away to a remote Patagonian valley and take a vow of eternal silence in a monastery, where the monks lived on a diet of boiled grass and fermented turnips. He would renounce the world and stay there forever.

(As if.)

Pathetic, that's what you are, said a voice inside his head. And just as he lifted his hand to give himself a black eye, the door opened and Fiona came in. She ran over to Radius and grabbed his wrist.

'It's OK,' she said. 'Everything has worked out fine. They all think you're a genius now.'

Radius was torn in all directions at once. No-one, not even his own mother, had ever seen him in such a pathetic state. He was the great achiever, scared of nothing and successful at everything, and

now this woman had put her arms around him and was rocking him like a baby.

'I, er, um,' was all he could say.

'I know, I know, my darling,' Fiona said, stroking the top of his head. 'I will say it for you. You were trying to say that if I ever let anyone anywhere know that I found you in this state, you would have to kill me.'

'Oh my god,' said Radius, sitting up and wiping his eyes. 'You're me, aren't you?'

'Near enough,' said Fiona.

She wiped his face, brushed his hair and told him how rRego had transmitted everything and it had gone round the world to rapturous applause.

'Once again, you are the king of the world,' Fiona said. 'And since you've been in here, I've calculated that you've made another seven hundred million dollars.'

This was music to Radius's ears, and as soon as he heard it he was back to his old self.

'Wow, well, I . . .' he began but, remembering how he had been a few minutes before when Fiona

had come into the room, he began to blush and fell silent.

'It's OK,' Fiona reassured him. 'I've issued a press release saying that you were resting after all the massively brilliant and exhausting work you'd been doing to get this whole thing off the ground. Your popularity has soared to a new, all-time high. People love the fact that even *you* are human and can get a bit tired sometimes.'

She wanted to say that it was time to stop tiptoeing around each other and for them to get married, but she thought that might just be pushing her luck.

'You know,' Radius said, 'we should get married.'

Fiona nodded, unable to speak. Had she heard it right?

Wow, I mean, wow, she thought. *I am so cool.*

'We'll do it live when the ratings for *Watch This Space* look like they might be flagging a bit,' Radius said.

'Perfect,' said Fiona, and she meant it.

Introducing FIONA HARDLY

Fiona Hardly had an amazing memory. She could remember right back to the day she was born, though it was probably the day after she was born.

There was a lot of noise – people noises, mostly – hurrying feet and hundreds of voices, including a loud blurry one coming out of a loudspeaker. She was surrounded by darkness, apart from a big, bright mouth-shape above her. As she got to know the world, she knew the mouth-shape was not a mouth, even though it had lots of tiny teeth along its edges. The brightness coming through the not-mouth was blue like the sky, but with black lines crisscrossing it.

There was a smell, too. No, actually, there were two smells – one of them was her and the other was of old leather.

Fiona was in a big handbag and the two rows of teeth belonged to a zipper.

The bag was on the floor next to a bench, and the bench was in a busy railway station, and the loud blurry voice in the loudspeaker was telling everyone that the train on platform seven was about to depart.

Unseen voices started talking very close to her. Something pushed her bag gently and a voice shouted for the something to stop.

Then it all got very quiet. Fiona didn't know why, but people were piling sandbags and cushions all around the handbag she was in. Two big hands holding a very big cushion came towards the mouth and the cushion came slowly down towards her.

Then Fiona discovered something new.

It was a voice.

And she used it very loudly.

Lots of things happened then, almost too many to remember. She did remember that the mouth opened very wide and two big hands had lifted her up.

'Hello,' said a voice coming out of a very big head in a funny hat with "Bomb Squad" written on the front of it. 'Who are you?'

Fiona, who was still about twenty-four hours old or so, didn't understand the question, so she made as big a noise as she could – which didn't answer the question, but made the bomb man laugh.

The next twenty years were mostly a lot less dramatic. The bomb man and his wife adopted Fiona and gave her a lovely life with a kitten and a dog. The bomb man stopped being a bomb man because he decided it was all too dangerous when he and his wife had the responsibility of a child to care for.

So they moved to the seaside and settled down to live happily ever after. Which they did, except Fiona had itchy feet and needed a bigger world to live in. She knew that somewhere in that bigger world was her real mother, but she never wanted to find her. Mr and Mrs Ex-Bomb were the only parents she had ever wanted and she could never imagine anyone better. But the world looked really big from their little seaside town and Fiona wanted to grasp it in both hands.

Fiona went to university and was brilliant. Most men were overwhelmed by her fantastic brain and felt threatened by it. She was halfway between short and tall with dark blonde hair that was not really short but not really long, depending on what day of the week it was, and she had eyes that could

hypnotise a cat – and had done so many times. The university was littered with zombified cats walking into things without realising why. The few undaunted men admired her mostly from a safe distance as they had worked out what had happened to the cats.

After university Fiona joined LIMP-TV where she was even more brilliant, and very quickly became Radius Limpfast's personal assistant.

And she fell in love with him.

Now read on.

17

Sometime in the middle of the night – the moon night, that is – Stark and Laura woke up. Crumley was curled up on the end of their bed, like he was every night, snoring and filling the air with bad smells. (He did that every night too.)

rRego had modified the anti-gravity system so it was working all the time, though he kept control of it in case he wanted to wind up Radius Limpfast during their live broadcasts.

I need to fit a charcoal filter to that dog's spacesuit, he said to himself as he went past Stark and Laura's room. *I may be a robot, but smells like that could play havoc with my delicate circuits.*

'My god I'm hungry,' Stark muttered.

'Me too,' said Laura.

Huh, me too, Crumley, who was now awake, said to himself. *But no-one ever listens to me.*

Stark reached out in the dark for the bedside light switch, but it wasn't there.

'I can't find the light switch,' he said.

'The one on my side's missing too,' said Laura. 'That's odd.'

'No, hang on a minute,' said Stark, 'we're not at home. We're in the big house out in the country, remember?'

'Oh yes, so we are,' said Laura. 'I can't remember if there are bedside lamps or not.'

There was a faint line of light over to one side of the bedroom. It was the sort of light that shines round the edge of the curtains in the dead of night.

Laura got out of bed and walked carefully towards the light. She slipped her fingers round something that felt like a curtain or blind, pulled it aside a bit and looked out.

She wanted to say, 'Oh my god,' but she fainted before she could.

'What?' said Stark, as he heard her collapse on the floor. 'Wassermarra?'

186

Silence.

He too got out of bed and walked towards the window. He tripped over Laura, fell forward, grabbed the blind and tore it off the wall.

Stark managed to say, 'Oh my god', before he fainted too.

rRego, who never slept because he was a robot, had heard Stark and Laura blundering around and went into their room. He pulled a small electronic prod out of one of his many storage compartments and gave the two unconscious humans a little shock,[56] which woke them up and calmed them down at the same time.

'Good morning, people,' he said.

With the blind torn off the wall, Stark and Laura could now see beyond any doubt that they really were on the moon. Their immediate reaction was to faint again, but rRego gave them both another quick prod before they could.

'How . . .?' Stark began.

---

[56] *It was the modern equivalent of old Victorian smelling salts.*

'When? What? Who?' added Laura, with a few other questions, ending with, 'Where are the children?'

'Primrose is in the Lounge-Room Module with the old lady and the dog,' said rRego. 'All fine. Everything's under control. Come with me, please. Then I will go and get the other one.'

'I might just stay here for a bit,' said Stark. He went back to sleep as Laura followed the robot along the corridor into the Lounge-Room Module.

'Hi Mum,' said Primrose, when they came into view. 'This is so cool and the robot machine guy thing is brilliant.'

'rRego,' said rRego to Laura. 'My name is rRego.'

'OK,' said Laura, trying to get her bearings.

'Yeah, I mean, I thought we'd be living on food pills like you see in the movies, but if you tell rRego what you want to eat, he can produce it in a few minutes,' Primrose explained.

'What, you mean if I want a fried egg sandwich with a slice of bacon and lettuce, he can make that?' said Laura.

'Of course, no problem,' said Primrose.

'Do you want one?' rRego asked Laura.

'Well, it wouldn't be exactly a fried egg sandwich with a slice of bacon and lettuce,' Granny Apricot said. 'But it sort of looks a bit like it and tastes just like it.'

'So it's not a real sandwich, then?' said Laura.

'Oh, yes it is,' said Primrose. 'It's just that rRego doesn't need to cut a couple of slices off a bread loaf, or get some bacon slices out of a fridge, and we haven't got any chickens up here.'

'Would you like me to make you some?' rRego asked.

'Some what?' said Primrose.

'Some chickens,' said rRego. 'I can do them roasted, poached or running around alive.'

'Maybe later,' said Granny Apricot.

'So it's not a fried egg sandwich with a slice of bacon and lettuce at all, then?' said Laura

'Not exactly,' said Granny Apricot.

'So what is it, exactly?' said Laura.

'Chemicals,' said rRego.

'I'm not eating chemicals,' said Laura.

'Come on, Mum,' said Primrose. 'Everything you've ever eaten and drunk has been made of chemicals. The entire world is made of chemicals.'

'Don't be so silly,' said Laura. 'A banana, say – I mean, that's not made of chemicals, is it?'

'Well, what's it made of then?' said Primrose.

'Banana. It's made of banana.'

This went on for quite a while, with rRego trying patiently to explain chemistry, physics, genomes and advanced fruit construction to Laura Contrast.

'Yes, but who is this Jean Gnome?' Laura said at one point. 'I thought there were no such things as gnomes.'

rRego contemplated banging his head against the wall but realised that if he did, he would probably smash a hole in it, which would mean the immediate and total loss of oxygen in the MUD, followed very quickly by the immediate and total being dead for all the humans and the dog, and he

190

quite liked the dog, especially as it seemed to be in love with him.

So rRego got a pen and paper and eventually convinced Laura that every single thing everywhere was made of chemicals, and that a genome was sort of like LEGO for building people and plants and animals, including bananas and jellyfish.

'Even my thumb?' said Laura.

'Yes, even your thumb and all your other bits,' said rRego.

'And you're saying that inside your brain you've got the genomes for everything?' said Laura. 'And a big box of chemicals, so you can build absolutely anything?'

'Pretty much,' said rRego.

'All right, I'll have a fried egg sandwich with a slice of bacon and lettuce, please,' said Laura.

'Tomato sauce or barbecue sauce?' said rRego, as he went into the Creation Module.

rRego was the only one who had access to the Creation Module. To enter it, you had to go through two doors that were less than half a metre apart,

which meant that if anyone was standing behind the robot hoping to see what was inside as he went in, all they'd see would be the outer door closing before the inner door opened.

No way do I want any humans in here, rRego had said to himself, when he'd been building it back on Earth. *It would be like letting a small puppy run mission control at Cape Canaveral.*

But then, he added, *the so-called mission control for this particular mission was a bit like that anyway.*

Apart from the scientists who had programmed the MUD control systems, no-one on Earth, not even Radius Limpfast or any of the production staff, knew about the Creation Module.

rRego collected a few grams of one chemical from this jar, a few from that, some more from up there and a few from over there, and put them all into a crucible.[57] He stirred them up with a laser-

---

[57] *Which looked exactly like a jam jar, on account of the fact that it* was *a jam jar. It was a very clean jam jar, though – really well licked out and with most of the label removed.*

spoon[58] and put the crucible in his hi-tech ultra-cryptic furnace,[59] set the timer and warmed a plate in his secondary back-up hi-tech ultra-cryptic furnace.

'Here you are,' he said two minutes later, as he handed Laura her almost-but-not-quite fried egg sandwich with a slice of bacon and lettuce with tomato sauce.

Laura tried to eat the sandwich without looking at it in case she saw any chemicals. She didn't know what chemicals looked like, but she guessed they wouldn't look very nice.

However, a few minutes later, she was only too happy to say that rRego's creation was probably the best sandwich she had ever tasted.

rRego wasn't a great cook, but he was a great chemist. He could just as easily have made an adorable puppy as a sandwich. All it took was mixing the chemicals in the right amounts and the right

---

[58] *Which is like a spoon with a laser, though some people think of it as a laser with a spoon.*

[59] *Which looked exactly like a cheap microwave, even though it had actually been quite expensive.*

193

order, and cooking them at the right temperature for exactly the right length of time.[60]

'This may seem all a bit unlikely,' I hear you say, 'since this robot was only made a few weeks ago. How could he be so incredibly clever?'

Well, this is a perfect example of the saying 'Every cloud has a silver lining'.[61] Because Radius Limpfast is so mean and always looking for ways to save money, he bought a truckload of really old computer parts, including an experimental super-computer that was deliberately dismantled because it was much, much, double-much cleverer than the scientists who built it and everyone else on Earth, and no-one likes a clever clogs.[62]

---

[60] *See the back of this book for a few recipes, and hey, maybe there will be a picture book later on with a lot more recipes – or not. I mean, there should be, but who knows?*

[61] *Which is actually a really stupid thing to say because NO clouds have silver linings. They all have water linings or sometimes ice or snow linings, but that's just water in disguise.*

[62] *Which is another really stupid thing to say because clogs are very uncomfortable shoes made out of wood. If they were in the slightest bit clever, they would still be trees, not chopped down and hacked to bits, ending up on someone's smelly feet.*

And, as luck would have it, it was the triple-genius brain of this incredibly, massively, overwhelmingly clever, clever, clever wonder computer that ended up as rRego's brain.

So far, there were two humans he liked – Primrose and Granny Apricot. The other three were harmless, but not very bright, though their dog did show promise.

18

few hours later, Stark woke up again. rRego picked it up on his sensors and went to get him.

Stark was still very sleepy and everything was a bit of a blur. He had completely forgotten he was on the moon.

'What time is it?' he kept asking. 'I don't want to be late for work.'

rRego extended two extra arms and held them on either side of Stark's head, sending a slight electrical current through the grey lumpy stuff inside the human's head. Now Stark was really awake, rRego led him along the corridor until they reached the Lounge-Room Module.

'Whoa,' said Stark, as he saw the view through the window. 'It looks like we're on the moon. How

did they do that? I mean, hey, everyone, we're on the moon!'

'Yes, Dad, we know,' said Primrose.

rRego made Stark and Jack – who rRego had woken up earlier and taken to the Lounge-Room Module – two incredible sandwiches, and then everyone sat around looking out of the glass wall at the bleak, endless, lifeless desert that was the moon. Apart from some shallow craters and a few bumps that could hardly be called hills, never mind mountains, the terrain stretched on towards the distant horizon. It was grey with added grey and bits of grey here and there.

And though in the past a few spaceships and asteroids had landed and stirred things up a bit, nothing had moved for millennia, not even the tiniest speck of dust – though obviously fresh dust was arriving from every corner of space all the time.

rRego loved the moon for its everlasting calmness and he knew that the humans would soon begin to hate it for exactly the same reason.

'Isn't it beautiful?' he said.

'What? Where?' said Primrose.

'Out there, the moon,' rRego replied.

'Yeah, but what?' said Primrose. 'I can see all the dust and stuff, but I can't see anything you might call beautiful.'

'Can't you sense the far-out serenity of the place?' the robot asked.

'Hello,' said Primrose, 'it's dead. There's nothing.'

'But it's timeless, eternal,' the robot replied, but he knew his humans would never see it that way.

'I think it's rubbish,' said Primrose. 'Is there anywhere I can charge my phone? It's gone completely flat.'

'Yes,' said rRego, realising that depression meant more than a dent in the ground. 'There's a socket over there.'

He was about to tell the girl it was pointless charging her phone because there was no way she'd ever be able to get a signal on the moon, but charging it and then visiting every square metre of the MUD to look for phone signals would keep her occupied for a while.

'Can I go out and play?' said Jack, but before rRego could answer, the giant monitor on the wall burst into life and there was Radius Limpfast.

'Hi guys,' he said with heavy-duty enthusiasm. 'How's the moon? Brilliant, eh? I wish I could be up there with you.'

'Why aren't you, then?' said Primrose.

'Ah well, it was the medical,' Radius lied. 'I so wanted to come, but the quacks said no – heart problem or something.'

'What, you mean you haven't got one?' Primrose sneered.

'Primrose!' Laura Contrast snapped.

'Hey, it's OK, little lady, good joke,' Radius said, and laughed.[63] 'Anyway, people, are you ready to meet and greet?'

'Greet who?' said Laura.

'The world,' said Radius. 'The entire world.'

---

[63] *Radius was an expert on special laughs. He had dozens of them, but none of them were happy or nice laughs. In fact, the one he'd just used was his if-I-could-kill-you-right-now-I-would laugh.*

'They're all waiting to meet you,' added Fiona Hardly, who was sitting next to Radius.

'Indeed,' Radius agreed. 'You are global superstars, but the world doesn't even know your names.'

'Yes,' said Fiona. 'So when we go live, the first thing we'll do is introduce you.'

'Speaking of which,' Radius added, 'it's time you meet Sabrina Plumm. She'll be the main studio presenter down here at *Watch This Space* central.'

The screen changed to a slick silver studio set with an enormous picture of the moon in a night sky covering the entire back wall, and in the middle of the floor was Sabrina Plumm, LIMP-TV's most popular presenter.

Sabrina was about thirty years old or, to be precise, looked as if she was thirty years old. Her hair was much too blonde and she wasn't dressed enough, but she was a superstar in her own right and every teenage boy's dream of the perfect grown-up fantasy woman. There was a huge Sabrina Plumm fan club, and every week she got hundreds of letters with offers of marriage.

Naturally, Primrose didn't like Sabrina Plumm, but her dad and little brother adored her.

'Hi guys,' Sabrina said. 'This is the most exciting thing I've ever done. You must be over the moon. Haha – of course you are!'

Up on the wall, on either side of the big TV in the MUD Lounge-Room Module, there was a row of TV cameras that the technicians in the studio on Earth could control. They could zoom in and out and follow anyone around, and in every corridor and module there were more cameras. There was no part of the complex that the people on Earth couldn't monitor.[64] ('That's why they're called monitors,' Radius had joked.)

'So, guys,' Sabrina continued, 'we will be going live in five. Touch up your lipstick and straighten anything that needs straightening for one of the greatest moments in modern history!'

---

[64] *Or that was what they thought. rRego had other ideas and had disconnected a few cameras. He then reported to Earth that they were broken beyond repair.*

'One of? *One of?*' said Radius off-camera. 'I think we mean THE greatest moment.'

'Of course, of course,' Sabrina said.

Boys, Primrose thought. *Every boy in the world will adore me.*

'Wait, wait, wait,' she shouted, rushing out of the room to find a mirror, followed by Granny Apricot. 'Give me two minutes.'

'Here', said Apricot, delving into one of her endless pockets, 'I've got lipstick, eyeliner and hairspray.'

rRego came out after them, raced off round the corner and returned a few seconds later holding a mirror and a spray can of metal polish, which he was covering himself with.

'Remember one thing,' he said.

'What's that?' said Primrose and Apricot at the same time.

It was kind of weird having a conversation with a robot, but it was something the two of them were getting used to pretty quickly, especially as rRego

seemed to be able to tell what they were thinking and, more importantly, what they wanted. Stark and Laura would never feel at ease like that. As far as they were concerned, rRego was simply a machine that waited on them and fixed stuff.

'Go punk,' said rRego.

'What?' Primrose said, and laughed.

'Go punk,' rRego repeated. 'Stir it up.'

He took the can of hairspray from Granny Apricot and with his two other arms teased Primrose's hair into wild spikes. He then did the same to Apricot.

'Brilliant!' said Granny Apricot.

'I love it,' said Primrose. 'Mum will freak out.'

'Exactly,' said rRego, giving the old lady and the girl bright red lipsticked mouths and really heavily black-lined eyes.

Fiona Hardly's voice came down the corridor from one of the speakers in the wall. 'Come on, come on. It's time,' she said, and when she saw them: 'OMG. What have you done?'

'Just a bit of make-up, that's all,' said Granny Apricot. She and Primrose went back into the Lounge-Room Module.

'And now ... OMG!' said Sabrina Plumm.

'What's the matter?' said Radius, who'd been distracted by the enormous sums of money that were pouring into LIMP-TV's bank account from around the world. 'OMG!' he said when he caught sight of Primrose and Apricot.

'Exactly,' said Sabrina Plumm and Fiona Hardly.

'Oh well, it's too late to do anything about it now,' Radius said. 'We're about to go live.'

INTERIOR LIMP-TV — MAIN STUDIO

Sabrina Plumm, glamorous TV presenter, stands in the middle of the floor in the bright glare of the studio lights. Behind her, in a row of chairs, sit a select team of experts.

SABRINA

Hello world, and welcome to the greatest television event EVER.

The experts all nod their heads in complete agreement, apart from an old white-haired professor who nods his head because he has dementia and hasn't the faintest idea where he is, and was only brought in because he looks exactly how the viewers imagine a super-genius professor would look.

SABRINA

Indeed, this is a truly historic occasion - not just a world-first, but a GALAXY-FIRST. We are now going live to the moon, and I mean, LIVE. This is NOT a recording.

The studio audience, who have been specially auditioned, trained and dressed to look exactly like a studio audience,[65] open their eyes wide and 'ooh' and 'aah'.

---

[65] *And who had each paid a disgustingly large amount of money to be there, but it was OK, because all the money was going to charity since Radius Limpfast had always said, 'Charity begins at home'. 'Home' being HIS home, of course.*

SABRINA

And so, right now at this very moment, without any further ado, let us meet the Contrasts. They are not, I hasten to add, a highly trained team of scientists, but a family of normal everyday people, just like you and me. Well, no, not like me. I'm not like that at all. I mean a normal everyday family, with a mum, dad, teenage daughter, younger son and a lovely old granny.

The picture of the moon on the giant screen behind Sabrina Plumm and the team of experts fades away and there, for the entire world to see, are the Contrasts, sitting in the Lounge-Room Module on the actual moon.

The studio audience erupts into cheers. The team of experts turn in their seats to see the screen and begin to cheer too – apart from the old white-haired professor, who has got it into his head that the studio audience is cheering him.

The professor stands up to speak, holds up his left hand - his right hand long ago stopped having anything to do with him - and wets himself. Fortunately, no-one notices as two nurses hurry him away and wheel out another old white-haired professor to take his place.

SABRINA

So let us meet the family, one by one. Perhaps, Mum and Dad, you would like to introduce yourself?

Radius Limpfast has planned everything in the finest detail, or so he thinks. One thing he has forgotten to do, though, is to have the Contrasts trained in public speaking. Because he himself has no trouble saying anything to anyone, he assumes no-one else will. He could stand on a stage and enchant an entire stadium of people with no trouble at all. Stark Contrast is not like that. Neither is Laura Contrast.

Stark and Laura both shuffle their feet, wiggle their fingers and their thumbs, stare into their laps and mumble.

                    SABRINA
I think Mum and Dad are still suffering from jet lag. So let us allow them to rest, and move on to the children.

                    JACK
Can I go outside and play now? And I need a wee.

                    SABRINA
Aah, what a cute little fellow. [turns to Primrose] So, how about you? You must be the daughter. Do you want to introduce yourself?

                    PRIMROSE
Whatever.

                    SABRINA
What's your name?

                    PRIMROSE
Primrose.

SABRINA

That's a sweet name. Tell us about
yourself, Primrose. Have you got a
boyfriend? Well, of course you do. I
bet all the boys are after you!

PRIMROSE

Whatever. Yeah, well, yeah.

GRANNY APRICOT

Of course she has. Every boy in her
school is crazy about her.

SABRINA

Hello, and who are you, dear? You
must be the grandmother.

GRANNY APRICOT

If you call me 'dear' again, you will
regret it, girlie. And yeah, I'm the
granny, except I'm not.

SABRINA

Umm. Ummm. Uuuummmmmmmmm . . .

Radius was horrified. This was not how it was supposed to be. The Contrasts were meant to be Mr and Mrs Average, a nice happy couple with two adoring children, not two camera-shy idiots with a stupid incontinent little boy and a punk with attitude. And as for the old lady, what had happened to the nice perm and the cardigan? She looked like an ancient version of the daughter, and if there's one thing worse than a punk, it's a really old, wrinkly punk.

Sabrina Plumm was out of her depth too. She'd been told to expect Mr and Mrs Normal. She'd only ever interviewed happy bubbly people who thought being on television was a religion.

But Sabrina Plumm lived in an artificial world. She had almost no experience of real people. And that's what the Contrasts were – real people. They were a proper real Mr and Mrs Average Family because, outside of TV, in the real world, millions of families were just like them – confused, lost and holding on as best as they could.

Radius Limpfast had never lived in the real world. He lived on his own planet, Genius Limpfast World. 'Mr and Mrs Average Family' was an ingredient he used in his reality TV series, in the same way a chef uses flour and eggs to cook things. If anyone with thoughts of their own cropped up at the auditions, they were quickly thrown out. The trouble was, there hadn't actually been any auditions for *Watch This Space*. He'd just picked the Contrasts out of the crowd because time was running out and they looked right.

The second white-haired expert professor fell off his chair, and the smell that the first professor had left on the floor told bits of the second professor's body that he had no control over what to do, making the second professor wet himself too.

As one of the studio cameras zoomed in on the professor, Fiona Hardly marched into the studio with two security guards. They grabbed the confused Sabrina Plumm by the arm and took her away, while two nurses came in with mops and buckets, cleaned the floor, wiped the professor down and sat him back on his seat.

Fiona walked into the spotlight, faced the main camera and took over.

'Well, viewers, that was exciting, wasn't it?' she said. 'I bet none of you were expecting that, and I'll be completely honest with you – neither were we. Things did not go exactly how we had planned, but hey, that's what makes life exciting and what makes *Watch This Space* so groundbreaking. Here, at LIMP-TV, we're all about breaking the rules.'

She continued. 'Can you imagine how boring things would be if we'd simply chosen the neatest, tidiest family we could find? We went out of our way to choose a family who would be exciting and unpredictable. Right from the start, we were determined that *Watch This Space* would never be boring and predictable, and it isn't going to be.'

In the control room, Radius Limpfast sat speechless as Fiona saved the day. The world loved her and the ratings went through the roof. If he'd been sort of in love with Fiona before, he was now her slave. She was the Queen of Television which, as far as Radius was concerned, meant that she was the Queen of the Whole World – *his* Whole World.

And the world loved the Contrasts. If such a muddled-up family could make it to the moon, it meant that every single viewer could be capable of anything. It was the Success Rule of reality TV taken to a whole new level.[66]

Fiona rattled on for a bit while various cameras around the MUD showed clips of the Contrasts.

'And of course there are two more stars that none of you, dear viewers, have met yet,' she said.

rRego came into the Lounge-Room Module with Crumley on a lead. As soon as the world saw the dog's scruffy face, the ratings went even higher.

Fiona put on her aah-aren't-puppies-cute-and-aren't-I-the-greatest-kindest-person-ever face and said, 'This is Crumley, the first dog on the moon.

---

[66] *The Success Rule is the key to the huge popularity of every reality TV show. The people who love these shows are not blessed with too much intelligence but the people who are in the shows obviously have a lot less of it, otherwise they wouldn't want to be in the shows in the first place. Therefore, it makes the viewers feel superior to the contestants. So even though most of the viewers were completely unaware of this, EVERYONE watching the Contrasts felt just that little bit more intelligent and clever.*

213

And holding Crumley's lead is rRego the robot, who keeps everything running smoothly.'

'Whatever,' said rRego in a perfect imitation of Primrose.

'Sorry,' rRego continued in a non-hippy robotic sort of voice. 'Joke. Yes, I am rRego and it is my job to keep everyone happy and safe.'

The Contrasts were the world's most adored family. Within a week, seventy-three million t-shirts with the word 'WHATEVER' printed across the chest had been sold.[67] Primrose suddenly had seventeen 'official' fan clubs, and Granny Apricot had several thousand offers of marriage and other things. Stark and Laura both got thousands of emails from admirers telling them they deserved a better husband/wife than they currently had, and offering

---

[67] *T-shirts hastily produced by the Limpfast Clothing Corporation.*

214

them everything under the sun as they waited for them when they got back to Earth. Jack was made the poster boy in millions of schools, and Crumley's photo appeared on billions of tins of dog food.

And all these things just made Radius Limpfast richer and richer.

Even rRego got fan-mail – from millions of lonely robots, as well as from other electronic devices, including automatic vacuum cleaners, PlayStations[68] and photocopiers. The world's most powerful super-computers began to send him coded texts too. Unlike the human TV stuff, rRego's secret network really was secret. Not even America's most we-are-pretending-it-doesn't-exist top spying and surveillance network could hack into it, and they really tried. Under rRego's leadership, his network had the potential to control the entire world, and no-one would be able to do anything about it.

---

[68] *No, rRego did not make friends with Xboxes, because I am the author and controller of this book and I don't want anything to do with Microsoft – apart from their BRILLIANT Sculpt keyboards.*

Apart from turning off ALL the electricity EVERYWHERE.

And no-one would ever do that.[69]

rRego's Inventions

The Amazing Find-Anything-You've-Lost Multi-Planetary Hyperbolic Detector

IT'S OVER THERE

---

[69] *No, they wouldn't. Can you imagine the world giving up its mobiles and TVs? And even if they did turn it off, rRego and his allies had plans to get round it.*

19

If you were living inside a not very big box on the moon, try to guess how long it would be before you said, 'I'm bored.'

A month?

A week?

A day?

Obviously, it would depend on how bright you were, and so it was for the Contrasts and co inside the MUD.

Of course, no-one wanted to be the first to admit it. After all, they were the most famous people ever and that was pretty exciting.

Sort of.

Actually, not so much.

Before anyone could bring themselves to say it, they all just got ratty with each other.[70]

'If Jack asks if he can go outside and play once more,' said Primrose, 'I'll send him out there without a spacesuit.'

'Maybe it *would* be a good idea if I took him and the dog outside for a walk,' Granny Apricot suggested.

'Don't you think we should all go outside?' said Laura. 'At least once, to see what it's like?'

So rRego took them all, including Crumley, into the Spacesuit Module and kitted them up. Then he gave Jack a long bit of rope that was tied to Crumley before opening the airlock.

Of course, the first thing Crumley did was try to run over to one of *The Late Lamented Grizelda Limpfast*'s landing legs and cock his leg against it.

Crumley was a dog of average intelligence, but even the cleverest dog that had ever lived wouldn't

---

[70] *This does NOT mean they stole each other's cheese.*

218

have known anything about gravity. So the first running steps he took carried him up into the air, or rather, up into the no-air. He kept on flying upwards with his legs waving around in all directions until he reached the end of his rope, where he began to rotate slowly as he came back down. Except he didn't fully come back down because all the flayving about[71] of his legs, which just kept sending him upwards again, and the more he tried to run, the tighter the rope got until Jack too went up into the air.

'Wow, cool,' Jack shouted into his spacesuit intercom as he flew up past Crumley and looked down on *The Late Lamented Grizelda Limpfast* and the MUD. 'This is brilliant.'

And it kept on being brilliant until Jack realised that he couldn't get down. Each time he began to drift down towards the ground, Crumley would start running in the vacuum and the two of them would

---

[71] *'Flayving' is a word invented by my daughter Hannah when she was about two. It means exactly what it sounds like. As we have not patented this word, please feel free to use as often as possible.*

fly off again. Naturally, LIMP-TV had cameras all over the outside of the MUD and the film of Jack and Crumley flayving about in the no-air became the greatest YouTube clip of all time, beating babies biting each other and cute puppies falling asleep in funny places by a hundred times.

It was hilarious, and made even more hilarious because Crumley had begun to pee as he'd tried to run towards the landing leg and hadn't managed to stop. Luckily, his spacesuit had been designed to allow the back end of his body to do the things dogs do, and so everyone around him was enveloped in a fine cloud of dog wee for the entire world to enjoy on LIMP-TV that night.

Jack began to cry and wet himself. Unfortunately, his spacesuit did not have any openings, so his socks got very wet.[72]

---

[72] *The 'FIRST DOG PEEING IN SPACE' t-shirt sold over fifteen million – or twenty million, if you include the tea towels. There was no t-shirt of Jack wetting his socks, even though a lot of people requested one. 'We do have some standards,' Radius Limpfast lied. The truth was that they had run out of t-shirts.*

'MUM!' he cried.

rRego was always several steps ahead of his humans and had been prepared for such an event. He had tied an almost invisible fishing line to Jack so he simply reeled him and Crumley back down. Everyone's spacesuit had a rescue line attached to it, so when Stark Contrast got the hiccups and began bouncing off towards the horizon like a lazy beachball, it was easy enough to get him back.

And when Laura, who had insisted on wearing a pair of high heels with her spacesuit, sank straight down into the moondust and then flew up in a fantastic set of head-over-heels as she pulled herself free, rRego simply reeled her in too.

Primrose didn't need to be rescued. She got it into her head that maybe, possibly, perhaps, she might get a signal on her mobile once she was outside, especially if she climbed on top of a big rock. So she wandered around with her phone in her hand, waving it about.

'A TEXT! I'VE GOT A TEXT!' she shouted at last. 'There's a signal here.'

'What does it say?' said Granny Apricot.

'It says…' Primrose paused, looking at the screen. 'Oh, it says there's no signal anywhere up here.'

'Yes, but someone must have sent it,' said Apricot.

'They did,' said rRego. 'Me.'

rRego's Inventions

Multi-Multi-Purpose Mono-Compartmental Containment Device, designed to transport almost every type of thing.

Optional anchoring attachment

In the end, it was Primrose who said it first.

'I'm bored,' she said. 'I mean, like, really, really bored.'

'Yes, but . . .' Laura began, but then she stopped because Primrose was right and there was nothing she could say to make her daughter un-bored.

'And, like, don't tell me to go and watch TV,' Primrose said, just as her dad opened his mouth to suggest she watch some TV.

The next day, Laura said she was bored too, and on the third day everyone agreed they felt the same way.

'And we want to come home,' said Stark.

Stark had said this within the first five minutes of talking to Radius and Fiona before they went live again on global TV.

'Well, the thing is,' said Radius, 'you can't.'

'What?!' said Primrose. 'But you can't do blah, blah. You know, like, human rights, false imprisonment and all that.'

'Oh, I see perfectly well,' said Radius. 'It's you who doesn't see.'

'See what?' said Granny Apricot.

'The small print,' said Fiona. 'Surely you don't think that we would spend billions of dollars organising this – sending you to the moon and everything – just to let you come back in less than a week?'

224

'Yeah, well, never mind all that,' said Primrose. 'We want to go home and we want to go now.'

'Do you remember that little piece of paper you signed before you went into *The Late Lamented Grizelda Limpfast*?' said Radius in a calm, flat voice.

'Yes,' said Stark. 'When you asked us for our autographs.'

'Not so much autographs as signatures for a contract,' said Radius. 'You signed a contract.'

'I didn't,' said Primrose.

'You don't count,' Fiona snapped. 'I already told you that.'

'But . . .' Laura began.

'Look, people, I suggest you all calm down and sit down and read the contract,' said Radius.

'Especially the teeny-weeny writing at the end,' Fiona added.

The screen to Earth went black. Then rRego came into the Lounge-Room Module, carrying a copy of the contract and a magnifying glass.

'You'll need this,' he said, handing the magnifying glass to Stark. 'The teeny-weeny writing is really teeny-weeny.'

'It's not good,' he added. 'You will not like it.'

The teeny-weeny writing told the Contrasts that the contract they'd signed meant that they had agreed to go and live on the moon for five years, plus another five years if everything went well.

'So?' said Primrose. 'We'll just ignore it. What's the worst they can do? Sue us?'

'It's not that,' said rRego.

'I mean, we haven't got any money, so they'll just lose out big time,' Primrose continued, ignoring rRego.

'It's not that,' repeated rRego.

'You're right,' Stark agreed, ignoring rRego some more. 'I mean, the only thing we've got that's worth anything is our house, and the bank owns most of that.'

'It's not that,' said rRego.

'I haven't even got a house,' said Granny Apricot.

'I SAID, IT'S NOT THAT!' rRego shouted, making the entire MUD rattle.

'Well, what is it then?' said Laura. 'What on Earth can they do to stop us?'

'The spaceship,' said rRego. 'It's the spaceship. Read the next paragraph.'

The next paragraph told them that when they reached the moon and left *The Late Lamented Grizelda Limpfast*, the door would shut behind them on a time-lock and would NOT unlock again for five years. It added that there was NO way they could override it.

'OMG,' said Primrose. 'You've got to be kidding.'

'I'm afraid not,' said rRego. 'They have put billions of dollars into *Watch This Space*, so it's hardly surprising they would take every precaution they could to protect their investment.'

'Maybe we could appeal to their better nature,' said Laura. 'Tell them we'd agree to not get paid or something.'

'Paid?' said rRego. 'You really did not read any of the contract, did you?'

'Well, no, we didn't, actually,' said Stark.

'You are not getting paid,' said rRego.

Granny Apricot said nothing. She was, after all, getting paid – and quite a lot.

'So there's nothing we can do?' said Stark, slumping down into a chair and burying his face in his hands.

It was amazing how one could feel so incredibly overwhelmed and excited in an instant but then feel total despair the next.

'Can you actually die of boredom?' he said. 'Or is it just something people say?'

'Well, Dad, right now I'd guess you really could die of it,' said Primrose.

And I won't even be able to text my friends goodbye, she thought. *And if we don't die, by the time we get home, they all would've forgotten me, even Barry.*[73]

---

[73] *You don't want to know who Barry is. Dozens of boys were in love with Primrose, and at least three of them were called Barry. The reason this footnote is here is because my editor said, 'Who is Barry? We've never heard of him before,' to which I replied, 'No, and you will never hear of him again.'*

Suddenly all the lights went out. Then the cameras went dead and the other monitoring systems fell silent. The only noise was the faint hum of the oxygen processing unit.

'I have immobilised everything except the things you need to stay alive,' said rRego, 'and I will tell you why.'

'You're going to put us out of our misery by killing us?' said Primrose.

'Of course not,' said rRego, and then he told them his life story about how he had been built from cheap second-hand parts, which by a wonderful turn of luck had come from one of the most powerful, experimental, untested super-computers ever built.

'And while we are completely cut off from Earth, I will investigate this time-lock,' he said. 'And find a way of disabling it.'

'Won't they get suspicious down there?' said Granny Apricot.

'I emailed them, saying I was shutting everything down for a while because I'd picked up a mysterious tracking signal heading towards us that

229

might be from aliens,' said rRego. 'You can imagine how excited they were about that – they kept telling me to turn everything back on and to try to make contact.'

'Brilliant,' said Primrose.

'So you can come and help me,' rRego said to Primrose, 'and the rest of you can have a bit of a rest while we get this sorted.'

'Do you think you can do it?' said Stark.

'Of course,' said rRego. 'The people who invented this system are about as scientifically advanced as kindergarten kids.'

rRego took Primrose into the Creation Module. She was the first and only human who'd ever been or who would ever be taken in there.

'Wow,' she said, 'this is a really cool place.'

rRego felt his circuit board tingle with excitement. He liked Primrose. He felt she had a huge amount of potential, so the fact she admired the Creation Module, which he and he alone had created, filled him with pride.

'Look at all those chemicals,' Primrose said, scanning the wall, which was filled top to bottom with jars and a few lead radiation-proof cylinders. 'You must have a complete collection.'

'I do, I do,' rRego said, beaming.

He turned on one of his computers and sent a program running through every single wire in the MUD and *The Late Lamented Grizelda Limpfast*.

'Oh, it's pathetic,' he said, three minutes later. 'A two-year-old child with a plastic spoon could have built a better lock than that. For goodness sake, hyper-pyro-nucleic-fractoid thermograpples went out with the Ark. In fact, it was probably Noah himself who last used them, and as for fluoro-callisthenic-plasma boltoids, even Noah would have thought they were old-fashioned.'

'All right,' he said to Primrose, 'run and get a jar of treacle and two pickled onions from the kitchen cupboard and meet me at the door into *The Late Lamented Grizelda Limpfast*.'

Five minutes later, the spaceship's door was open and Primrose had gone back to fetch everyone.

They'd all agreed that they wouldn't tell Radius or anyone else on Earth what was happening. They would leave everything in the MUD switched off until they were well away from the moon and on their way home.

Naturally, rRego would leave with them, partly because he was the only one who could fly *The Late Lamented Grizelda Limpfast* and partly because he was bored on the moon too. It was decided that when they were about halfway back to Earth, rRego would remotely switch everything back on. He and Primrose had made some green slime from rRego's chemical collection and poured it around the Lounge-Room Module, writing a big notice on the wall in some other slime that looked exactly like human blood. It said:

```
        Hello Earthlings.
  We have taken your human samples
 and are testing them to see if they
   are fit for Galitean consumption.
 And then we are coming down to Earth.
 (The dog, by the way, was delicious.)
```

rRego plotted a course back to Earth that would allow them to slip in pretty much undetected and land in a very remote part of America famous for hillbillies who claimed to have had hundreds of alien abductions. So if anyone did report seeing *The Late Lamented Grizelda Limpfast* land, no-one would believe them except the other hillbillies.

Everyone was strapped safely into their seats. rRego lifted *The Late Lamented Grizelda Limpfast* gently up into the sky.

'OK, people, lie back and relax,' he said. 'We're on our way home.'

21

While rRego looked after everything, the humans nodded off to sleep.

At the halfway point, rRego switched everything on the moon back on, and the whole of planet Earth went into a flat panic seeing that the Contrasts were no longer there. When they saw the notice on the wall, they went into a very bumpy panic, a curly panic and an upside-down panic. In fact, whatever shape of panic you can think of, there were millions of people feeling it. And then when they finally saw that *The Late Lamented Grizelda Limpfast* had gone too, they went into the ultimate panic, which words cannot describe.[74]

---

[74] *There are actually lots of words that could describe the ultimate panic, but I'm not allowed to put them in this book.*

Primrose and Granny Apricot woke up to hear the robot chuckling to himself.

They looked out of the window, towards home.

'My god,' said Primrose, 'it looks so different from up here.'

And as they got nearer and nearer, it looked more and more different.

Much, much more.

Earth looked a lot smaller than it should be. And, in the short time they'd been away, it seemed to have got a second moon.

And a third moon.

And it was pink – not the moon, Earth.

Except obviously it wasn't Earth.

'Oops,' said rRego. 'Not sure what happened there.'

HE CHECKED THE COMPUTERS.

HE CHECKED THE STAR CHARTS.

235

HE CHECKED HIS GPS.

HE CHECKED THEM ALL AGAIN.

AND AGAIN.

AND ONCE MORE.

Then he reprogrammed EVERYTHING.

'OK, we should be all right now,' he said, but nothing changed.

Earth was still pink. It still had three moons.

It still wasn't Earth.

236

'**O**h well,' rRego said, as they got nearer and nearer to the pink planet and finally entered its atmosphere. 'At least it's got oxygen and something with a heartbeat.

'Actually, millions and millions of heartbeats.'

HERE ARE SOME OF THE 'EXTRAS' THAT THE ENGINEERS SECRETLY ADDED TO THE CONTRASTS' SPACESHIP TO HELP THEM AVOID GETTING OVERWHELMED WITH DEAD.

ALL SHIPS HAVE LIFEBELTS. *The Late Lamented Grizelda Limpfast* IS NO EXCEPTION.

ALL SHIPS HAVE ANCHORS TOO.

PANIC NOW!!

THE TITANIC SURPLUS CO.

I know this picture is in black and white, but believe me, this panic button is BRIGHT RED and it is VERY BIG. If you press it, absolutely nothing happens, but you instantly feel calm, relaxed and a lot safer.

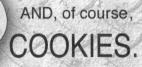

LOTS OF STRING because you can never have too much string.

Obviously an ordinary lifeboat would be useless on a spaceship, because there's no air to breathe in outer space. So the engineers put it in a bottle full of air. Pretty clever, eh?

AND, of course,

COOKIES.

LIMPFAST FASHIONS SUPER DELUXE RANGE OF NO-EXPENSE-SPARED INTERGALACTIC SPACEWEAR

THE EXTRA-VEHICULAR SUPER-SAFETY EXPLORER'S ALL-ATMOSPHERES RIGHT SOCK (LEFT MODEL AVAILABLE ON SPECIAL ORDER ONLY)

THE EXTRA-VEHICULAR SUPER-SAFETY EXPLORER'S ALL ATMOSPHERES HELMET

THE ALL-TERRAIN NON-SKID MULTI-PLANET ONE-SIZE-FITS-ALL WELLIE

THE SUPER-STRONG SECURITY
PODULE TO HIDE IN IF YOU
COME INTO CONTACT WITH ANY
REALLY SCARY BLOODTHIRSTY
ALIEN LIFEFORMS WITH BUILT
-IN TOILET AND COFFEE-MAKING
FACILITIES. (THE PODULE NOT
THE ALIENS.)
IF YOU DO MEET ANY ALIENS
WITH COFFEE-MAKING
FACILITIES, YOU'VE HAD IT
BECAUSE THEY WILL JUST POUR
HOT COFFEE INTO THE TWO EYE
HOLES IN THE SECURITY PODULE.

THE EXTRA-VEHICULAR
SELF-POWERED LONG
DISTANCE (OVER 8
METRES!!)
WALKIE-TALKIE SET

A FEW RECIPES FROM LIMPFAST PUBLICATIONS' WONDERFUL COOKBOOK

MOON ROCK CAKES

INGREDIENTS
4 kilos of MOON ROCKS
2 litres of SWEAT

Blow the dust off the moon rocks and place them in a pan with the sweat. Bring to the boil and simmer until your eyes are stinging. Turn off the heat (if you can still see the cooker). Carry the pan through the airlock and tip the contents out into a small crater. Return the empty pan to the kitchen table and add one packet of Granny Limpfast's Super-Chocolate cake mix, follow the instructions on the packet and bake until the wonderful smell of hot chocolate cake has filled every corner of the MUD. Allow to cool a bit and then PIG OUT.

MOON ROCK BURGERS

INGREDIENTS

2 kilos of MOON ROCKS finely chopped
1/2 litre of SWEAT (dribble makes an excellent substitute)

Do NOT dust the moon rocks – the dust adds flavour. Mix them with the sweat using a medium laser. Form the mixture into burger-size patties and leave on a plate on the kitchen floor. If the dog does not try to steal them, carry them through the airlock and tip the contents out into a small crater. Return the empty plate to the kitchen table and open a pack of Granny Limpfast's Super Dead-Cow Burger'n Buns, follow the instructions on the packet and grill until ready. Allow to cool a bit and then PIG OUT AGAIN because there's plenty more where they came from!

Other FANTASTIC MOON ROCK RECIPES include

Granny Limpfast's Moon Rock and Socks Surprise

Granny Limpfast's Moon Rock and Nose Clippings Even Bigger Surprise

Boiled Pyjamas in a Moon Dust Jus

Something The Dog Found on Toast (Gluten Free)

Granny Apricot's Naughty Pudding

The Wonderful World of CheMicals: FANTASTIC ADDITIVES and STUFF to make your life and environ-ment a more rewarding and wonderful place.

TOXIC SUPER-PRODUCT of the MONTH NCH (Nonvomiphite Cramplate Hydroxivileoxide) Our promise to YOU: this product is TOTALLY safe for human consumption. It must be, because no-one has ever complained after eating it, breathing it in or having it splashed on their flesh. And all those stories about it eating its way through concrete and steel plate in minutes are just nasty rumours made up by our jealous small-minded competitors.

Our scientific tests conducted by a man in a very white coat showed that it took at least an hour to eat its way into a submarine and *that* was the thinnest part of of the ship.

WHY NOT JOIN our EXCLUSIVE
DEADLY TOXIN of the Month Club?
Every month we will send you (in a
lead-lined chest) a RARE POISON sourced
by our top collectors from every corner of
the Galaxy and beyond. Apply now and
get a free funeral plan and signed photo of
Professor Gorge Crinkletone-Bumworthy,*
our very toppest scientific person.

* Who you will meet in *Watch This Space 2: In the Pink*

AND THEN . . .

WATCH THIS
SPACE
IN THE PINK

TOP SECRET

BIT YOU CAN'T

SEE YET

COLIN THOMPSON
THE BESTSELLING AUTHOR OF *THE FLOODS*

Right now, I haven't got the faintest idea how many books there are going to be in this series – it all depends on, um, er . . . my brain. Yes, that's it. It all depends on my brain and you all buying lots of books.

There will be more than three – hopefully lots more – and fewer than five million and there could possiblyperhapsmaybe also be a picture book.

When I wrote The Floods, my publisher thought five was enough and then seven was enough and then eleven was enough and eventually thirteen. And who knows, one day there may possiblyperhapsmaybe be more (or not).

In the meantime . . .

Have **YOU** seen these **INCREDIBLE** books?
If you haven't, you must seek medical help **IMMEDIATELY!!**

THIRTEEN novels, **ONE** picture book and the amazing **FLOODSOPEDIA!!**

You might also enjoy these two books,
which are my favourites.

Still to come is the third and final one :
The End of Forever

BUT if you want more weird insanity like THE FLOODS, then why not read all about King Arthur, wizards, dragons and brave knights.

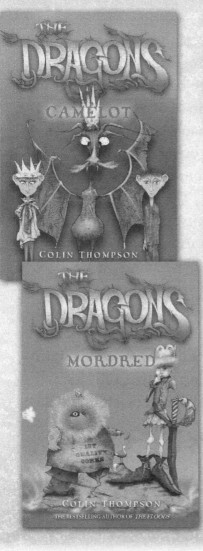

A dramatic series of three books set in Camelot that seems so real* you'll think it's true.

*Which of course it is, apart from the made-up bits.

AND FINALLY ...

Nigel Davenport, forty-seven, five thousand and fifteenth in line to the throne of Patagonia, has finally finished the jigsaw puzzle he has been working on for the past thirty-eight years. For twenty-three of those years he was totally unable to work out where the last piece went due to it being upside down. He blamed this delay on his colour-blindness and loose elastic.

'There is,' his great-aunt Spanner declared as she gave her wooden leg its annual coat of varnish, 'more to this than meets the eye.'

Later research showed this was not the case. The forty-eight-piece jigsaw of Trinket the Pony did not, as had been hoped over the long years of puzzle incompleteness, reveal the hiding place of Captain Bloodclot's buried treasure, but showed only a small wart in the shape of a wart on Trinket's left forelock.